Alpha Queen

Book 3
Shifter Royalty Trilogy

By: S. Dalambakis

Edited by Rachael Kunz of Muddy Waters Editing

Created with Vellum

To those of you who are taking this journey with me.

Now the story's played out like this,
Just like a paperback novel,
Let's rewrite an ending that fits.

"Someday" by Nickleback

Prologue

Callyn

I knew something was up when the boys let me walk to Max's by myself. Ever since the Kelsey incident and the fight, one of them has been glued to my side. The only time I get a break from them is when I go to the bathroom and when they have to leave my house for the night. My aunt Dahlia had to do an awful lot of convincing that I would be safe with just her guarding me before they would even think about leaving. At one point they were trying to convince her to let one of them sleep on the couch. She put a stop to that right away. Plus, there was no way any of their parents would have let that happen.

Color me surprised when I received that text from Max telling me to walk over to his house. I stayed hyper aware the whole ten minutes it takes me to walk there. I started using my shifter senses. Any sight, sound, or smell I don't recognize doesn't get past me now. After everything that has happened I would be a fool not to be prepared. I still haven't officially been christened the new Alpha Queen. I would bet money that everyone is waiting for the outcome of the impending war.

I wouldn't name someone my queen, just to have her perish in battle. You would end up right where you started, queenless. The smart choice would be to wait. I'm not sure I'm even ready for that title. I feel like haven't earned it. No, there is no question about that; I haven't earned it, but I will. If anything positive has come from everything that I have been through, it's that it's made me stronger. If I'm going to be their queen, then that is something that I need to continue. I need to learn how to be queen. My aunt Dahlia and Elder Harris said they would help me...us, learn what we need. My phone beeps signaling a text message.

Max: Move those little legs faster. I'm getting impatient.

I roll my eyes.

Me: Well, if you would have waited a minute, I would have been knocking on your door. I'm outside on your porch.

Not even a minute later, Max opens his front door and is standing in front me. A hum of appreciation escapes my lips. Blue jeans, an open red button-up shirt revealing a white tank underneath, and his signature long blonde hair completes his look.

"You know a ride would have been preferable. It is the middle of February," I chastise.

"I know, angel, but this is one time all of us needed to be together. Otherwise, one of us would have been there to give you a ride." I sigh. I can't even pretend to be mad at them. It never works. I can't stay angry at them long. "Come on inside before you freeze anymore."

I step into his foyer. I don't make it far before he tugs on my wrist and pulls me into his body. I love the feel of his arms around me. I feel safe, secure, and loved. I feel that way with all of them. They give me the strength that I need when I can't seem to find it for myself.

I look up into his blue eyes, there's a mischievousness to them, more so than usual. My body is flush with his. He gives me this half smirk smile. I follow his eyes as they gaze over my face, landing on my lips. It's a silent question he is asking me. One that he already knows the answer to. He graces me with a full smile before he descends. His lips press against mine. The kiss is quick and not at all what I was expecting. Normally, we would be making out in his hallway to the point one of the other boys would have to come searching for us. He can see the disappointment on my face when he pulls away.

"We'll have time for that later. But for now, I need you to close your eyes." I eye him suspiciously. "Trust me, angel; it's nothing bad." I roll my eyes and do as he ask.

"I swear, Max; if you're messing with me, I'll sick Graydon on you."

"Relax. I promise, I'm not messing with you." I feel his hands cover my eyes.

"What are you doing?"

"Making sure you can't peek." We walk slowly together his hands over my eyes, him guiding me. Suddenly, we stop. "Now keep your eyes closed until I say open." I felt him move his hands from my face, but I kept my eyes shut. "Open your eyes, angel," he whispers.

I slowly open my eyes.

"SURPRISE!"

I'm standing in the middle of Max's living room with my mouth agape. All the boys and their parents, my aunt, and Cat are here. There are two giant gold balloons in the shape of a one and eight in the middle of the room with dark blue and yellow balloons scattered around the living room. The furniture has been moved and sits along the wall, leaving the middle of the living room open.

"Wh-what is all this?"

"Did you think we would forget your birthday, sweetheart? You only turn eighteen once and you deserve a celebration," Zeke says as he walks over to me.

I'm embraced in his arms before I can say anything more. After my mother died, my birthday was no longer celebrated. I never did or went anywhere special. This is my first celebrated birthday in eight years. To be surrounded by the people who love and care about me, is everything. I can't hold in my emotions any longer, and I start to cry. Zeke pulls back enough to gaze at my face.

"No crying allowed today," as he wipes the tears from my face.

I smile, "It's my party, and I'll cry if I want to." He chuckles, the sound is like music to my ears.

"You got me there. Come on, let's go celebrate."

We did, and it was amazing.

Catori

I just got home from Callie's surprise birthday party. Let me tell you, it was so much fun ganging up on Max with her. Serves him right too, you can't go around picking on people and not expect retaliation. Maybe now, he'll think twice. Celebrating Callie's birthday is just what I needed to take my mind off of everything that has happened in the last couple of weeks.

Callie was there the night this strange entity appeared before us and gave me the power of having visions. I am now the new prophetess. Callie and her guys are happy about the change. I can't blame them after what Kelsey did. I have first-hand experience with her. She wasn't always like this, but something changed in her. To this day, I still have no idea what caused this reaction. We haven't seen or heard from her since the fight with the North Pack went down. There are a few still in town, but they have been model citizens. I'm going through the motions of getting ready for bed, when it happens.

Callyn is standing front and center with Lucian, Zeke, Maximus, and Graydon behind her.

"You can't win against us."

"See, that's where you're wrong. Even if I fail, there will always be someone to take my place," a faceless voice says.

"If that's true, we will stand up and defeat anyone who dares threaten the safety and livelihood of shifters."

A maniacal laughter fills the silence. "I don't plan on losing. You see, I brought some backup."

A figure walks forward removing the hood of the purple cloak they wear, revealing a woman.

"Who the hell are you?" Graydon questions.

"I'm Circe."

"Yeah, I'm gonna need more than that," Max says sarcastically.

"How about I just show you?"

Elbows at her sides, palms up, fingers bent, she starts to chant. Her head falls back, eyes closed. There is a white light that starts to build in her palms. The more she chants the brighter the light gets. Her eyes snap open, and she lifts her head. She moves her palms forward, facing Callyn and the boys. No warning was given before two orbs of white light are blasted, hitting Callyn and her mates.

It takes a moment but the light fades. A motionless Callyn, Zeke, Lucian, Graydon, and Maximus are left in its wake. The same evil laugh can be heard.

"Come Circe, our job here is done. Let's go make the world ours."

I come out of my first vision. "Holy shit."

Chapter 1

Callyn

Do you ever get the feeling that something bad is about to happen? Maybe it was the way Catori stood by my locker, or maybe it was the look on her face, but I knew whatever she was about to tell me, I wasn't going to like.

"Whatever you have to say just make it quick."

"How do you know I have anything to say? I could just be tired."

I tilt my head slightly to the side. "I can tell by your face. I mean your expressions always give you away."

"You got me there."

"Spill."

"So, the other night, after your birthday party, I had my first vision." I feel my eyes grow wide, and my mouth opens in shock. "Yeah, it was weird but there's more." I nod for her to continue. She sighs, looking down to the floor. "I don't know how to tell you this. What I saw...," she shakes her head. "You all die," she whispers.

"Excuse me, what?" There's no way I heard her right.

"You all die, Callie. I saw you and your boys die at the hands of a witch. There was someone else there, but I couldn't see his face. I could only hear what he was saying."

No, no, no, that can't be right. There's no way I'm going through all of this just to die. I didn't survive my father, no my stepfather, only to die. I didn't survive that barn fire, an abduction, and a battle to die now. I can't; I won't. I can hear male voices around me, but the sound of my own beating heart is drowning out everything they're saying. My chest feels tight like I can't get enough air. I can feel hands on me as the darkness clouding my vision tries to take me.

My body feels light. Slowly, my vision returns to normal, the tightness in my chest eases. That's when I feel their energy, each unique.

Graydon's energy is hot and powerful, Zeke's strong and balanced, Max's light and playful, and Lucian's grounded and warm. Their energy is helping me. I realize it's their hands I feel on me, surrounding me, protecting me.

"Come on sweetheart, say something, anything." I can hear the worry in Zeke's voice.

"She's got two seconds before I pick her up and haul her ass to the nurse."

"You have to keep calm, Graydon. This isn't helping her any." As much as Lucian was trying to keep everyone calm, I could still feel his anxiety. Snap out of it Callyn.

I take a deep breath, trying to steady myself. "I'm okay," I whisper.

"Oh, thank fuck, angel." Everyone gets quiet. "You had us so worried," Max says right before he envelops me in a hug. A second later, I hear his voice in my head.

Seriously angel, you scared the shit out of me.

I know, I'm sorry. I just started to freak out. I wasn't prepared for what Cat had to tell me.

What did she say that scared you this bad?

She didn't tell you?

No.

It was nothing good. I just need another minute, and I'll tell you all at the same time.

Take all the time you need, angel. We're not going anywhere.

We learned that while I can communicate with each of them telepathically, they can't with each other, and I don't project my thoughts to all of them. I have to concentrate on each of them individually. We hope that with time and the strengthening of our bond that we'll all be able to communicate with each other without having to try. It will come in handy when we have finally taken over. We would be able to talk telepathically and come to an agreement.

"Can someone tell me what the fuck is going on?" Graydon bellows. He's close to flipping his shit.

"She says she needs a minute. Damn, calm down; you'll get your answers. Callie, can you please tell us what happened before Graydon decides to go Hulk and start smashing."

I can picture it in my head. Graydon with his scowl, arms at his side, and hands balled into fists. I can see his chest heaving, moving more rapidly the angrier he gets. A giggle escapes my lips. This is what I need to shake the fear still clawing at my insides - to forget the words that Cat had said. A moment to forget about the impending future and enjoy my boys for just a moment. I take a step away from Max and mimic the way I see Graydon in my head.

I deepen my voice. "Graydon angry." I pretend to smash something in front of me. "Graydon smash." The boys and Cat start laughing. It's just what I need to calm me down further.

"Why you little," Graydon says as he stalks toward me. "You think you're so funny, don't you?"

I nod my head yes, while I bite my lip, trying to control my laughter and smile. He may sound serious, but I can see he's struggling to keep a straight face. I smile cheekily at him. I don't even move. I know he would never hurt me. He sighs, finally breaking.

"You're lucky you're so cute. I wouldn't take this from anyone else." I open my arms, and he walks right into my embrace. I love that I'm just tall enough to be level with his chest. I lay my ear right over his heart and listen to the steady rhythm. It calms me a little more. I feel him lay his cheek on the top of my head. He inhales, breathing in my scent which calms him. "Will you please tell us what's going on now?"

I take a deep breath and repeat what Cat just told me. A chorus of cuss words could be heard.

"How are we supposed to fight a witch?" Zeke questions.

"We find one of our own," Lucian states.

"How the hell do we do that? Do you know where to find a witch, because I sure don't," Graydon growls.

"Does anyone else feel like we are in over our heads?"

"I agree with Zeke. I don't know what I'm doing let alone know where to go from here," I state.

"I have an idea." We all look at Lucian. "I think we should get all our parents together. They have to have some idea. We can't do this alone. We'll need their help coming up with a plan and with contacting other shifters. We need to scour those journals again."

Max groans, "Not the journals again, anything but that."

I chuckle. I reach for Max's hand, interlacing our fingers. "How about we read the same journal."

"I like the way you think." He leans down and kisses my cheek.

With everything going on, these are the moments that I live for, that I will fight for.

Catori

As I watch Callyn and her mates, I can't help but be a little jealous. I'm jealous of their relationship and how the boys are with her. Hell, at this moment Graydon - who would rather kick your ass first and ask questions later- is pushing a lock of Callyn's hair out of her face. He cups the side of her face, rubbing her cheek with his thumb. His touch so gentle, so sweet. It makes me wonder about what my life would be like if Elijah was still here. Will I ever meet someone? Is there another destined mate for me? Will I find a love like theirs? I look away not wanting to spy on the private moment any longer.

I clench my fist. The more I think about it, the more I'm getting pissed. My anger is not directed at Callyn and her mates. No. This anger is reserved for Kelsey, the she-bitch. *She* is the reason I don't have my mate, and I have *yet* to make her pay for it. I will, one day.

"This is more information than we had before. We now need to take this information and one: tell our parents, and two: use this to our advantage. We make a new plan to counter this," Lucian says breaking my thoughts.

"As if all of us dying is an option," Graydon states as he crosses his arms.

"So, am I the only one wondering if Kelsey saw this. Obviously, she didn't tell us, but she had to tell someone. Right?"

We all stand there with our mouths open. I know we were all thinking it to some degree, but coming from Max, it leaves me a little stunned. I honestly didn't think he had any actual brain cells. Huh, you learn something new every day.

"What?"

"I never thought I would see the day that something intelligent would come out of your mouth."

"That's not the only thing that I can do with my mouth." Max looks over at Callyn and gives her a wink while he bites his lip. I hear her sharp intake of breath. I roll my eyes. It's Max. Ew.

"And just like that it's gone." I shake my head.

"Aww, don't be that way Kitty Cat. I've been known to have a good idea a time or two."

I roll my eyes. "Whatever. I'll meet up with you later." I give Callie a quick hug before I turn and walk down the hall to my first class.

We have grown close over the few months that we've known each other, Callie and me. I told her more about how my mate died, and she told me about how her life was living her dad, which turns out was just her stepdad and not her real father. She was there the night I became the new prophetess, and we've both talked about how scared we are by our new roles, not having any idea how to deal with them. We are literally winging it.

You would think there would be a manual somewhere. A How to Guide of being a prophetess and Alpha Queen. Some form of written archives. Ugh. *Stop this Cat. You are not a whiner. Get your shit together.* Maybe this is something that me and Callie can do with the help of her guys. History is doomed to repeat itself. Case in point our current situation. We are gearing up for a war, just like our last Alpha Queen. The only difference, it seems, is we have time to prepare, make a plan, gather forces.

What the hell do I... we, a bunch of eighteen-year old's, know about planning and fighting in a war? Nothing. This situation is so messed up. They have been lucky so far, but eventually that luck will run out. My first vision proves at least that much. I'm going to help Callie as much as I can. I won't be like Kelsey.

I'm so lost in my own thoughts that I don't realize I walked right past my first class. If it wasn't for the fact that I accidentally bumped into someone, I wouldn't have known. I turn around and walk back down the hall toward my class. Once there, I take my seat. I open my book bag, pulling out a leather journal and pen. I do this every time - pick up the journal, smell the leather and the parchment paper. Two of my favorite smells.

I've been debating on whether I should write any visions I have down. It could help in the long run. I pick up my pen and twirl it through my fingers. The blank page staring up at me. Screw it. I start to write, every little detail. There has to be something important in here. Something that maybe I don't understand but Callie or one of the boys might. I could totally be over thinking this, but my gut is telling me that there is more to this. There has to be.

Chapter 2

Maximus

I'm all for a seemingly fast school day, but I seriously don't want to read those journals again. Yeah, there was some useful information in them, about our abilities and such, but it's still boring. Yet, here I am sitting at Callie's with a big ass tome on my lap wishing it was Callie instead. I need to make that happen. Besides, she said we were going to read our journal together. I look over to the couch where she is sitting next to Lucian, lost in her own thoughts.

Man did I get lucky to have her as my mate. She's wearing black leggings, a teal t-shirt, and her long, red hair spills down her back from under a grey beanie. Wait a minute, that's my beanie. When did she take that from me? She looks better in it than I do. Besides, I shouldn't hide all this hair anyway. No one likes hat hair. She's biting her bottom lip. She really has no idea how beautiful she really is.

"Callie," I call. She looks up at me. "I thought you said we were going to read our journal together, and yet," I spread my arms out, "I find myself sitting here all by my lonesome." To top that off, I give her my best puppy dog eyes. You know what she does, she laughs at me.

"Max, you didn't have to give me the eyes," she says as she puts her journal off to the side. She stands up, walks over, and stops right in front of me. "Well, are you going to move the book, or are you just going to stare at me?" Then she has to go and give me that smile. The one I would do anything for. The one I live to see on her face every day.

"Both," I answer.

I close the book, keeping one finger on the page I was staring at for the pass half hour, because I was not reading this *again*. I move my arms out of the way. Callie understands what I mean. I'm so glad she doesn't hesitate and just sits right down on my lap. A few months ago, we never would have been able to get her to do this. Slowly, but surely, Callie is coming into her own.

"Happy?"

"Very." Neither of us could keep a straight face, and we bust out laughing.

"Alright, let's get back to it."

"Ugh, do we have too?" I whine.

"Yes, we have to be missing something. Lucian is waiting to hear back from his grandfather. I know a lot information was lost, but it doesn't hurt to try."

"I know, but I would rather be doing something else."

"Yeah, like what?"

"This."

I drop the journal and cup her face. I pull her face closer to mine, stopping just before our lips touch. I hear her breathing hitch. I don't waste another moment. The kiss is tentative at first, but then I nip at her lower lip, getting me exactly what I want. The second she parts her lips, I slip my tongue in. God, I love the sound of her moan. I could kiss her like this forever. The need for air has me pulling back enough to look into her eyes.

"Hey, what are you guys doing?" Callie's aunt Dahlia says as she walks into the living room.

Callie turns her head to answer when I feel her tense up. Is she preparing herself for the way her aunt is going to react?

"Hey," I bounce my knee to get her attention. When she turns to look at me I can see the fear in them. "What's wrong?" She starts to shake her head. "Tell me."

"We shouldn't have done that in here," she whispers.

"What? Kiss? Why?"

"Because the other guys are in here. I wasn't thinking. I shouldn't have kissed you in front of them."

"Why not? You can do whatever you want."

"It's not fair to them. They shouldn't have to see that."

"How about we ask them. Guys?" I say to get their attention.

"Max, please."

"No, we aren't doing this. I don't want you scared to show me or any one of them affection when you feel like it. Do you understand?" Callie nods her head. "Good." I turn my attention to the guys. "Do you care if Callie kisses me or one of you in front of the rest of us?"

"No."

"Of course not."

"Why would we?"

"Callie seems to think that she shouldn't do that in front of each other."

"Callie, we would never ask you not to be yourself and doing what you feel is natural. None of us is going to get mad," Lucian states.

In a move that surprises even me, Lucian gets up, walks over, and stops directly in front of us. Callie has to tip her head back to look up at him. In one smooth, swift move he gathers her hair in one hand, tugging, making her head fall back further. His other hand moves up and spreads out across her neck, keeping his thumb and index under her chin, giving him all control of her head movements. He leans down searching her eyes for something? What? The okay to do it? For her to say no? Whatever it was he found, because in the next moment, he presses his lips to hers. I see Lucian's fingers flex ever so slightly. It causes Callie to moan, opening her mouth, giving him the opportunity to deepen the kiss.

No part of me is weirded out by this. In fact, I find the situation hot. Callie is lucky that she is sitting sideways on my lap; otherwise, she would feel *just* how okay I am about this. Hmm, now this has possibilities. I smile at my thoughts.

Lucian

I pull back, staring at Callie's face. Her cheeks are flushed, eyelids partially closed as if waiting for more, the way her body leans toward me begging for more. It turns me on. It's taking everything I have not to find the nearest surface and continue what we're doing, but I know she isn't ready for that. Callie is better off being with one of the others first. I'm trying to gauge her reactions to certain things I do. Mostly, to make sure she has no sort of flashback or memories crop up of her stepfather. So far, so good. She has come a long way from that shy, quiet girl we met. She still has her moments of insecurity, like now, but we have been trying to show her she has no need for that. I hope my little display proved just that.

I know Callie is not the only one affected by what just happened. I can smell the lust coming off of Max. I notice Callie clenching her thighs together. Good. It's just the reaction I was hoping for. She handles my shows of dominance well by naturally submitting to me. She's not even aware that she is doing it. I know we're going to have to have a certain conversation soon, but I'm not and she's not ready for that yet.

"Any more doubts, baby?"

I see her swallow, trying to compose herself before she answers. "Nope, none."

"Good." I give her a quick peck on the lips before I release her and go back over to my seat. I look over at Zeke, who is just staring wide-eyed at me, which I understand. I'm not known for doing what I just did, but I felt like I needed to make a point, and I did. My eyes go to Graydon, who is death gripping the arms of chair he is occupying. "You good, Graydon?"

His eyes meet mine. They are flicking back and forth between his normal color and that of his bear. I can't tell if this is happening because he liked what he saw or because of the possessiveness of his bear. If I had to guess, I would say a little bit of both.

"Yeah, I'm good. I just need a moment," his voice coming out harsher than normal.

"Well, that was quite entertaining," Callie's aunt says. "This is on the list of things you never want to see." She shudders. "It's a little to much."

Well, if that doesn't help Graydon I don't know what will. Another first for me. I forgot she even entered the room. I look over at Callie to see how she is doing, and I can see the blush on her cheeks.

"Sorry, Aunt Dahlia," she says.

"Don't worry about it, you weren't doing anything wrong. However, I would like to know what you are looking for in the journals. Anything that I can help you with?"

"I don't know."

Callie goes on to explain the vision Cat had, and how we feel like we are missing something in the journal.

"You think there is a clue as to whom might have been in the vision?" Aunt Dahlia questions.

"I don't know. I've looked at the journals, multiple times, but I haven't found anything. I pretty much have a photographic memory, but I thought maybe I missed something the first few times I've looked through them,yet I haven't found anything new."

Aunt Dahlia's brows furrow. She's staring at the space in front of her, almost like she is trying to recall some detail. Then as if a light bulb goes off she looks up at us with a shocked expression on her face.

"A witch. We need a witch. One, because the witch can be there to help fight off the witch from the vision. Who better than one of her own kind. Second, remember when I told you your mother had a witch come in and put a block on your powers?" Callie nods. "Well, what if that's not the only thing that she did, what if she had her put some sort of spell on the books?"

"We came to the same conclusion earlier, that we would need a witch to combat a witch. Do you really think it's possible? That the books could be spelled?"

"Yes, I do."

"Is there any way you can get ahold of the witch?" I question.

"I can try. It's been years since I've seen her, but I'm hoping she's still in the same area as she was back then."

If Aunt Dahlia can find that witch, we just gained a leg up on trying to change that vision.

Chapter 3

Callyn

Finding that witch has been harder than we hoped. It's been a week and still no word. At this point, I would take any witch that could help us. I mean they all have to know the same sort of spells. Right?

"Earth to Callie," a hand waves in front of my face. "What's going on in the pretty little head of yours?" Max questions.

"I was just thinking about the witch, wondering if they all know the same spells and if we could just use any witch, or do we have to find the one that my mother used because she originally placed the spell."

"Actually, that's a good question," Zeke states.

"The only problem is who the hell do we ask? I would think that the only one that could answer that question would be another witch, but I don't see a plethora of witches we can ask," Graydon growls.

I sigh, "I know." I turn and focus on Lucian. "How about your grandfather? Do you think he would have any more luck?"

"I could ask, but I don't know how much help he can give us right now. You know he's been swamped since half the council turned out to be against us. He's been taking over for all of them. Plus, the lessons he's been giving us, so we can eventually take over, he's stretched thin."

"Is there anyone else we can ask for help?"

"I honestly can't answer that. It's hard just trying to figure out who we can and can't trust."

"I know, but how much longer can we wait. We don't know when or who the next attack will be, and you know there will be more."

"Okay, can we stop the doom and gloom talk before it really begins," Max says.

"Unfortunately, no. This isn't the time or place for it, but a serious discussion on our next steps is definitely needed. We can't be caught unaware like we were last time," Lucian states.

"I would rather be prepared, than not. Cat being the new prophetess is the best thing that has happened. This is a first step in the right direction. We now have time to plan; we didn't get that luxury with Kelsey," I say.

"Speaking of the she-bitch, has anyone seen or heard from her since the stunt that she pulled?" Max questions.

Everyone shakes their head. I don't know if that's a good or a bad thing. A part of me hopes that she stays in hiding, ashamed of what she has done. But, I don't know if Kelsey can actually feel that emotion. If I had to guess, she is probably still plotting against us. I highly doubt that she sees what she did was wrong. I don't want this to go to war. I don't want to see anymore bloodshed over this, but I know that I'm not going to get my way.

The only thing that I can do now is prepare for what is to come. We all do. Yeah, Lucian's grandfather is helping us understand the politics, but we're eighteen years old. Who is going to take us seriously? Who is going to listen and abide by rules set by eighteen year old's? No one. That's who. No one in their right mind is going to listen to us. So, we really have our work cut out for us. Lucian's grandfather thinks that this war will help us. This will be our first real test as leaders and the outcome is everything.

No pressure, right?

Just win a little thing called war, and that will appease the masses. I inwardly groan. You know, if someone would have told me that this is what my life was going to be like, I would have laughed. The shy, quiet girl in school is the Alpha Queen. I have not one, but four mates, who I love and love me. They are the best part of all this. They keep me going. I don't know what I would do without them.

"Well, wherever she is, let's hope that she stays there," Graydon says.

I couldn't agree more, but we all know that won't happen.

I'm sitting on my bed, doing my homework, when I hear a knock on my door. A second later, my Aunt Dahlia pops her head in, opening the door.

"Hey, you think you can text the boys and have them come over? I have some news for you guys, and I want to tell you all together."

"Sure, is everything okay?"

"Yeah, everything is fine. Actually, there is someone coming that I would like you to meet." She must see the confused look on my face and decides to stop with the mystery. "I found a witch, and she says she might be able to help us."

"Where did you find her?"

"Actually, I've known her for awhile. She's more of an acquaintance."

"Do you trust her?"

"I believe we can. She hasn't given me any reason not to."

"Well, damn. I'll message them now. When is the witch going to be here?"

"Should be any minute. They don't need to drive anywhere. They have the ability of snapping their fingers and transporting themselves wherever they want. A neat trick really." She shrugs her shoulders. "I'll see you downstairs."

I pick up phone and send out a group text.

Me: My aunt found a witch; she should be here any moment. Come over when you can.

Zeke: We'll be there in a few minutes.

Graydon: I'll drive. Meet me at my house.

Max: Do you think she has a cauldron?

Lucian: Really, Max? Just get to Graydon's.

Lucian: On our way, baby.

I let out a sigh. I hope this witch can help us.

Graydon

This witch better have some answers. We're beating our heads against the wall at this point. Something's got to give. I know we aren't showing it, but the vision has all of us shook. Even me. I will do whatever I have to, to make sure that Callie is safe. It doesn't take long for everyone to pile into my truck. I think we were all in motion the moment we got that text.

"What do you think of this? Do you think we are going to get some answers finally?" Zeke questions.

"We can only hope, but at this point what else do we have to go on?" Lucian answers.

Not another word is said as I drive the few blocks over to Callie's house. I pulled up on to the driveway, none of us wasting time getting out.

We go up the stairs and knock on the front door. Callie answers with a smile on her face. "Hey guys."

Callie moves to let us past as I go I place a quick kiss on her lips. If she is going to get rid of any doubt about us being fine with seeing her give all of us affection and attention, then we need to do the same with her. I move over to the side to let the rest of the guys in. Zeke follows and does the same thing I do. Lucian tugs on her hair before he gives her a kiss.

"Come on, you guys are taking too long I want my turn," Max whines.

Callie chuckles as Max picks her up and spins her in a circle before giving her a quick kiss. Instead of putting her back on her feet, he carries her into the living room.

"You know I can walk right?"

"Yeah, but this is more fun." She rolls her eyes but smiles.

No sooner after we all pick a spot to sit, you could feel the pressure in the room change. In a blink of an eye, there is a woman standing before us. She has black hair that reaches her shoulders in an array of messy curls. Her skin is the color of mocha, flawless, and her eyes are the brightest, violet I have ever seen. They are framed with thick lashes, black eyeliner, and mascara. She has on a high-waisted, pleated, ankle length, grey skirt. Her top is off the shoulder, simple, and black. She has on strappy, black high heels. She's a beautiful woman, but I don't trust her. How did she magically appear in this room?

"Who the hell are you?" I growl, getting up so I can move closer to Callie. I'm not the only one.

"My name is Alcina, and I'm the witch who's going to help you."

"And just how do you plan to do that?"

"I'm going to take a look at the journal and see if there is more to it. I will be able to sense the magic. After that, I will help aide you in the oncoming war."

"Why would you do that?" Callie questions. "You don't know us, so why would you help?"

"One, beggars can't be choosers. You clearly need my help; otherwise, why would your aunt have contacted me? As far as I can tell, I'm the only witch here. Are you really going to turn away my help? And two, I don't want this war to happen. But, I know that it is. Do you honestly think that the world, or shifters for that matter, will be better off in the hands of whoever your enemies are? You got a taste of that a couple of months ago, the Elder Council. That was a dictatorship waiting to happen or try to happen at the least. They were never going to succeed."

"Care to explain," I growl.

"Someone else was giving the council orders. Well, a few of them anyways. It's always easy to spot the power-hungry ones," she says with a shrug, like it's no big deal.

"How do you know someone was pulling their strings?" Max asks.

"Come on, you can't really be that dense. There is always someone bigger who needs underlings to do their dirty work. Case in point, to get rid of you five. You are the biggest obstacle and threat to whatever they have planned."

"So, are you trying to tell me you're Glinda the Good Witch and you're going to help us defeat the Wicked Witch of the West? How do we know you won't betray us?" Max questions.

"You don't, but I'm hoping that by me helping you along the way that I can gain your trust. I'm going to start doing that by helping you with the journals."

Callie sighs, "Fine, I'll go get them."

"I'm coming with you," I utter.

I make sure I place myself between Callie and Alcina. No way in hell am I giving this unknown witch easy access. I follow Callie up the stairs and to her room. Neither of us speak until we close her bedroom door behind us.

"What do you make of her? Do you think we can trust her?" Callie ask as she starts to pile some of the journals on her nightstand back in the box with the others.

I sigh, "You know me; I don't trust anyone, and it's even harder for me to trust anyone after what we all went through, you especially. We are going to have to keep an eye on her, and one shifty move from her and she's done."

Callie turns to look at me. "Okay."

"Okay?"

"Yes, okay."

"I expected you to fight me about that."

"Not about this. Don't get me wrong, I'm still going to argue with you but not about this."

I walk up and wrap my arms around her. "Are you ready for this?"

"Not really, but who is? I wonder if she knows the witch from Cat's vision, and if she does, maybe she can help us stop her?"

"Maybe."

She tilts her head back to look at me. I love the smile she gives me. I lean down and place my lips on hers. What's supposed to be a quick chaste kiss turns into something more. She moans, and it's the best sound I've heard. I'm so focused on Callie, that I don't hear the door open.

"Ahem. Am I interrupting something?"

Max.

Callie giggles. "I guess we were taking too long."

"I guess so."

"We should get back downstairs. Can you carry the box downstairs for me?" she asks as she pats my chest.

"Yeah," I grumble.

"Thank you, grumpy bear."

Callie steps around me and toward the door. She stops in front Max and gives him a quick peck on the cheek. Max swats her butt before she can move away.

"Behave."

Callie leaves me and Max standing in her room.

"Pay back," Max says with a smile. I take a step toward him, but he laughs and ducks out the room. The bastard. I pick up the box and head down the stairs after them.

Zeke

I watch as Callie, Max, and Graydon walk back down the stairs. This whole witch thing is crazy. We have to be crazy, right? After that vision of all of us dying, we have to be more careful about who we give information to. The whole thing with Kelsey and Elder Council already has us going out of our minds with worry over who will be coming after us next. And the longer it takes for the next attack, the bigger it will be.

I eye the witch again, as Callie makes her way over to the couch and sits next to me. Max takes the chair that Graydon normally sits in. Graydon places the box on the coffee table in front of Callie and sits on Callie's other side, the two biggest guys taking post to protect her.

Alcina moves forward and places a hand over the box. "Yes, I can feel the magic. At least one of those journals has been altered."

"Do you think you can break whatever spell is on it?" Callie inquires.

"I won't know unless I try."

Callie looks at me, then to Graydon, followed by Lucian and Max. She gives us a slight nod. "Okay, why not. What can it hurt?"

We watch with eagle eyes as Alcina starts to pull the journals out of the box one by one. She's about half way through when she stops; her hands just hovering above the next journal.

"This is it? Are you sure?" Zeke questions. I nod my head.

"I'm going to warn you now whatever this journal holds maybe of no use to you. At least it may not help you with this coming war," Alcina states.

"Well, we've come this far; no use turning back now. Besides, why place a spell on the book if it holds no useful information? There's something in there that they wanted to hide."

Alcina carefully pulls the journal out of the box. Graydon and I quickly clear off the coffee table. She places the book down in the center. All of us are waiting, glued to what she is doing. Her eyes are closed, and she is muttering something underneath her breath. Both of her hands, palms down, are spread across the journal. There is a soft white glow that emanates from her hands. This goes on for a few minutes and nothing happens. Well, as far as I can tell nothing happens.

"So, did it work?" Graydon says with a slight attitude.

"Let's open it and see." Alcina flips through a couple of pages before she stops at a blank page. She utters another spell and words start to appear, well like magic. "Hm, it looks like only a spell spoken by and a drop of blood from the Alpha Queens line will reveal its secrets."

"I don't know any spells."

"We can start by placing a drop of your blood on the page and see what else appears. The spell may be hidden in the pages and only activated with the blood."

"No, absolutely not," Graydon growls.

"I don't think I have a choice. This seems to be the only way." Callie looks at Alcina. "This is the only way, right?"

"Yes."

Callie sighs, "Okay, let's get this over with."

With a wave of her hand, Alcina conjures a needle.

"Well, that's a nifty trick," Max says.

"Your hand please." Callie lifts her hand and places it palm up in Alcina's. A quick prick of her finger, Alcina turns it over and squeezes until a single drop falls onto the page. You can feel the ripple of magic spread across the book. "There should be a spell." Alcina turns the journal around and faces toward Callyn. All of us scoot closer. "Just speak the words that are on the page."

"What words?" I say.

Callie looks over at me. "You don't see them?"

"No."

"Hm. Very clever. It seems the witch that placed the spell made it only visible to the Alpha Queen or the heir. I can't see the words either, but I felt the magic. At least we know you are the legitimate heir to the throne."

Callie reaches up and pulls her necklace from beneath her shirt. "Like this wasn't enough. Oh, and by the way, I shift into a phoenix."

Alcina nods her head. "That necklace is legend. It's part of the stories that are told to us as children. I never thought I would see it up close."

"Can we just do this? There will be time for all of this later," Graydon says angrily.

"Geez, take a chill pill," Max states. "Go ahead Callie; we don't need Graydon hulking out."

Callie takes a deep breath before leaning forward to peer at the book.

"A drop of blood is all takes for you see the hidden spell inside of me. The words spoken for you to hear will also make what you can't see clear. This only works for those with the right gene for I am the rightful Alpha Queen."

The pages of the book start to flip back and forth rapidly before finally settling down. All of us scoot even closer together. There is not an inch of space that separates us. The first page is a picture of talisman. The center is a blood red, hexagon shaped stone that is surrounded by a Celtic star. Callie turns the page and in big, bold, black ink is a name; Lorcan Camden.

"Why does Camden sound familiar?" I ask.

"Because... that was my mother's last name."

"Well, damn," I whisper.

Chapter 4

Callyn

Zeke couldn't have said it any better. I look to my aunt, who has been surprisingly quiet through all of this, and to Alcina. I have a feeling I know where this is going. But, I need to hear it out loud.

"Lorcan is a relative of mine, isn't he?"

"Yes," they both say.

"How exactly is he related?"

"He was the brother to the last Alpha Queen, making him your great-great-uncle." Aunt Dahlia answers.

"I don't remember seeing him anywhere in the family tree journal."

"You wouldn't have. That journal only followed the Alpha Queen line. Her brother was never going to see the throne. He would have had his own journal made of his lineage. None of the information that was passed down to me mentioned him having any children or even a mate."

I look back to the journal to see what else was written underneath his name. The more I read the less I liked about him. How he murdered and slaughtered innocent shifters. How he degraded them by hanging them from trees. For what? Power? To rule? All of it was needless. We can only hope that he didn't procreate. He would have passed down all his hatred and jealousy, and we would have even bigger problems.

"He killed his sister. Didn't he?" I whispered.

"Fucking hell," Graydon growls.

"Did you know?" I ask my aunt. "How about you, Alcina? Did you know?" I was practically yelling at this point.

"I didn't know," Alcina answers.

"Everyone had their suspicions, but nothing has ever been confirmed. All the records from then were mostly lost. It had to be chaotic when everything happened. There were fires, buildings destroyed. No one would have been worried about saving such things. Getting out alive and keeping their families safe would have been the most important thing. "

"Well, someone had to know. Why else would it be in here?" My brows furrowed in confusion. I meet my aunt's eyes. "When you first told me about what was passed down to you from your family, about the night the Alpha Queen died, you said the handmaiden only left with the baby and a sack of coins. Is there more to the story that you didn't tell me, or that I didn't read in those journals?"

"Of course, there is more to the story. There is always more to the story. There whole reason we have that journal is because at some point the Alpha Queen slipped it in one of the pockets of her handmaidens dress."

"Why didn't you tell me your ancestor found a journal in her pocket? When did she find it?" I hear Graydon scoff beside me. He isn't any happier about this situation than I am.

"It didn't seem like that information was important, at the time. She found it after the ship had set sail. At least, that's what has been passed down generation after generation."

You know, I think we need to start looking for information ourselves. This is bullshit. How does anyone except us to win a war if they aren't telling us everything?

I look over at Graydon. I understand where he is coming from.

I understand but I don't know what to do.

We branch out and do this ourselves.

We ask Lucian, we say at the same time. I chuckle.

What are you two doing? I look at Lucian.

Well we were going to ask you later to help us come up with a plan on how we can do this without anyone's help. We both think this whole thing is bullshit.

Not a bad idea. My first bit of advice is to not read any more of that journal until you are alone or when all of us are alone. I don't trust anyone but us.

Good point. I sigh.

"What did I miss?" Alcina ask.

"They can communicate with each other telepathically."

"Interesting. And you can do that with all of them?"

"Yes."

"You are going to be powerful indeed."

"And right there is the reason why we can't trust anyone. Are you going to pretend to help us and then when you have the perfect opening screw us over?" Graydon bellows. "What happened to finding the witch that originally put the spells on the journals? Where is she? Why are you the one that is here?"

"The original witch died, a long time ago. Witches do have an extended life span, like most supernaturals, but we don't live forever. You were never going to be able to find her. I'm here because Dahlia asked me to. I'm here to help, whether you believe it or not."

"Graydon," he turns his head toward my aunt. "I've known Alcina a long time, and while we may not be best friends, I do believe she has your best interest at heart."

"I'll guess we'll have to wait and see," he states.

I wish Cat was here. Maybe if she touched the witch, she could get a reading on her like Kelsey did with you when she touched your necklace.

I look at Zeke. *I can message her and see if we could set something up.*

It couldn't hurt to try.

I focus on Max. *Hey.*

Yes, angel.

Do you want to help me trap the witch so Cat can try to get a read on her?

Like you have to ask. Any time I can cause mayhem, you know I'm down.

I smile and shake my head.

Awe come on. You know I like to help.

I can't lie. *I do.*

Max smiles at me, then winks, and pushes his hair behind his ears. Man, do I love my guys.

"So, what's our next move?" Zeke asks.

I close the journal and cradle it to my chest. "I'm going to take this journal and go through it again now that there is no spell blocking it. Alcina, are there anymore journals in the box that have been altered with magic?"

"Let me check." We watch as Alcina moves to the box and hovers her hands over it. "No, the rest are clean."

"Great. Graydon, can you carry the box back up to my room?"

He grumbles but gathers the box and the books. "Lead the way, Callie bear."

I focus on each of them, *Let's go.*

Without question, each of them gets up and start to follow me. I stop at the top of the stairs before turning back. "Thank you Alcina. Is there any way I can get ahold of you if I have any questions?"

"Yes." With a wave of her hand a piece of paper floats down to me. I catch it. "My phone number. Until next time, my Queen." With a snap of her fingers Alcina is gone.

"Still a really cool trick."

"Shut it, Max."

"What? It is. Even you have to admit that it would come in handy."

"You only want it, so you can get away faster after you prank someone."

"Yeah, you're right."

I just shake my head. "Come on, let's go do this."

Lucian

Callie sits in the middle of her bed. Max is lounging back against her headboard, Graydon is sitting on her computer chair, Zeke is sitting on the floor in front of her bed leaning back on it, and I'm perched on the edge of her bed. We're all listening to her read from the journal.

"June 1st, 1818. There has been whispers around the castle that my brother is planning to overthrow me. He has been gaining followers. The things he is telling them are lies. Why can they not see that? There is another rumor, he has found a witch to make him a talisman. Lorcan wants to gain power and fast. This talisman is said to draw magic inside it. If that is the case, we are all going to be doomed."

"Do you think the talisman is the one pictured?" Zeke asks.

"Yes. The question is, is it still out there?" I answer.

"If it is, then who would have it?"

"Callie, flip through and see if it says what happened to the necklace."

It takes her a few minutes. "The last mention of the talisman is from an entry on July 31st, 1818. My end is drawing near. I can feel it. The rumors are true about my brother, about everything. I know he plans to kill me. I've stayed hidden in my castle the last few months. My brother and his spies can't find out my secret. I will do whatever I can to keep my baby safe. I need to find a way to get Lorcan's talisman and destroy it. I fear that is the only way to save myself, my family, and all of shifter kind."

"Clearly, she didn't succeed," Graydon states.

"Flip to the last entry and read what is says."

"September 2nd, 1818. No matter what I have tried, I can't seem to overcome my brother. It's just a matter of when he is going to attack. We have taken measures to try to ensure our safety, but I fear it may not be enough. He has grown in power, so much so, I believe he is now stronger than my mates and me. We planned an attack on his followers, but no matter how many we seem to get rid of, more appear. I don't see a way out of this. I have to make sure my baby survives, that she is safe. We built an escape route in our bedroom. My mates wish for me to take our daughter and run, but I can't. What kind of queen would I be if I didn't stay and fight? No, I will not run as much as I would like to. I have made my peace that I will not watch my daughter grow up. My only wish now is that when I send her away, she learns of me and her fathers."

Callie sighs.

"I really hope the other entries in this journal turn out to be more helpful," Graydon grumbles. We all look at him. "What? Those entries didn't tell us anything we didn't already know. The Alpha Queen died, the handmaiden escapes with her baby, and that talisman is out there somewhere. How are we going to find that? Because I, for one, don't want that falling into the wrong hands. Who knows, that vision Cat had, that mysterious voice, he could have it already. Or that damn witch."

"Shit," Max whispers.

"I'll finish reading the journal and let you know if I find anything useful," Callie says.

"We can always use Alcina." Everyone looks at me. "I know that you and Max were going to plan something."

"We would never," Max scoffs.

"Are you sure you can't hear us when we talk silently?"

I smile. "No, I can't hear Max, and I only hear you when you project to me. But, we all know that you like to help Max with his little pranks."

"Little," Max says affronted.

I smile bigger. "Yes, little. You can't deny it. We know that's exactly what you would do. But, I have another idea. If there is nothing in there about the whereabouts of the talisman, we ask Alcina if she would use a location spell or something along those lines to find the necklace. There has to be some kind of magic to help with that, right?"

"Let's hope."

"Alright guys, it's getting late. Let us know if you find anything, baby." I lean over, tug on her hair, and give her a quick kiss. The rest of the guys follow suit.

Graydon waits until everyone is in his truck before he speaks. "Great, instead of getting answers, we got more pieces to this messed up puzzle."

"We'll figure this out. We have too."

Callyn

This journal, while nice to have, hasn't yielded any significant information so far.. I went back to the last page I was reading, before the guys had me skipping around. I read through more than half of the journal before I found something that could help us. Well, sort of.

July 28th, 1818,

We have come up with a plan. We need to destroy the talisman, then all of my brother's power will be gone. With no powers, he will lose everything. Lorcan cannot defeat me or my mates. He needs that talisman. One way to know for sure that it gets destroyed is by having a witch use a spell. We don't know of any other way. It took us some time, but we found someone willing to cast the spell for us. Circe. She should be here in a couple days' time. Then we can put an end to this once and for all.

Crap. Wasn't Circe the name of the witch from Cat's vision? What happened? How is she still alive? I flip to the page and then next. I keep reading until I come across the journal entry that explains what happened.

August 15th, 1818,

We have been betrayed. Circe played us like a fool. She led us to believe that she was on our side, but everything we told her, she went back and told Lorcan. We now have to come up with a completely different plan. I don't know what we're going to do. We don't have time to try to find another witch, and even if we did, there is no way of knowing if they would be on our side. I just don't understand why Circe didn't kill us herself? Unless, my brother has truly gained enough power. I shudder at the thought. We did learn that the power he is gathering is coming from around him. Mother Nature. The very thing we all need to survive. We noticed that when we try to draw small amounts of magic, to help with controlling our elements, it's weak. We are weaker as well. I fear that even if we had a witch on our side it's too late. I fear Lorcan is too powerful for us, any of us, to defeat. God help the shifter race.

I grabbed my phone and opened the group text.

Me: Guys! I found something.

Lucian: What did you find?

Graydon: And

Zeke: What it is, sweetheart?

Max: Don't keep us waiting, woman.

Me: First, I need to make sure of something. Lucian, can you tell me the name of the witch from Cat's vision?

Lucian: Circe.

Me: I thought so. In a journal entry, Camila mentions that they were going to get help from a witch. One guess on who that witch was.

Graydon: Circe.

Me: Ding, ding. The problem is Circe betrayed Camilla. Circe was a spy for Lorcan.

Lucian: Did it say anything else?

Me: Just that he was gathering magic from nature and she knew he was too powerful. Camilla knew she wasn't going to win that fight.

Zeke: So that talisman is still out there in the hands of someone else. Someone we don't know.

Lucian: Yes.

Me: That's not the only problem.

Max: You mean there's even more bad news? Ugh.

Me: Unfortunately, yes. Circe was alive two hundred years ago. How is she still alive today? And does that mean that Lorcan is still alive as well?

Lucian: Are we sure it's the same person? Could it be a descendant and she is just named after her?

Me: I don't know. I think you're right Lucian, but I think we need to be prepared for anything.

Max: I foresee us speaking to a witch in the near future.

Max: Guys, just so you know you should read that last text in a Zoltar voice. You know the fake fortune teller machine, because that's totally how I said it in my head as I typed it.

Graydon sends the eye roll emoji, Zeke the face palm emoji, and Lucian just a simple 'smh'. I laugh because I can picture each of them doing exactly what they texted. Man, I love these boys. We may not have all the answers right now, but we will. We won't stop until we do, and we win.

Chapter 5

Maximus

You know, I've come to realize we have no luck. I mean absolutely none. We get more questions than answers, more problems yet no solutions. I hate being Debbie Downer, but something needs to turn around. I know all of my friends think I'm just a big ball of fun, and I am, but I'm more than that. I can have good ideas and thoughts. Like now, well I don't know if they would consider it a good idea. In this case it's more of a question.

"Hey guys." Everyone turns and looks at me. "So, I was thinking about our text message conversation from the other day and I was wondering..."

"Just spit it out already," Graydon grumbles.

"Chill out, I'm getting there."

"Well, get there faster."

"Fine, Mr. Impatient. I was wondering how are we going to find who has the talisman. I mean Lorcan had to give it to someone, right? But, who would he give it to? There had to be someone he was close to or at the very least trusted enough."

"Actually, that's a great idea. I think our best option will be to contact Alcina. We have to test her loyalty at some point and what better way. Plus, I'd like to know sooner rather than later if she's going to betray us," Callie states. "I'll contact her as soon as I talk to Cat. I want her there as well. It can't hurt to have another set of eyes of Alcina."

"Well, now that has been established, I have one more question, but this one is just for Callie." I wait until I have her attention, which doesn't take much. She gives each of us her undivided attention when we are speaking to her. I wait just long enough to pique her interest and to annoy Graydon. "Callie, will you go out on a date with me?"

I see the shock on her face. It's the one thing we haven't done one on one. We always do things as a group, and I'm cool with that; it's just I want to spend some time with her by herself. Callie isn't the only one that is shocked. The rest of the guys are wearing similar expressions. I can't help but smile. I beat them to something for once. I put my focus back on Callie, eagerly awaiting her answer. Luckily, she doesn't make me wait long.

"I would love to go out on a date with you," she says. I love the smile she gives before she launches herself at me. I laugh as she squeezes me in one of the fiercest yet happiest hugs. I hug her right back.

"Good. Friday night, it's a date."

Callie steps back and giggles. "I can't wait to tell Cat."

That has to be the girliest I've seen Callie act since we've meet. The bell picks that moment to ring. Callie grabs my hand and practical skips us down the hallway.

"Um, angel?" She stops and looks at me. "You do realize that we don't have the next class together, right? My class is on the other side of the building." She cocks her head, thinking.

"My bad." She shrugs her shoulders. "I was so caught up in the moment that I didn't think about it. But you better go before you are late to class." She steps forward, gets on her tiptoes, and gives me a quick kiss.

"Hell, I don't mind being late for class if you're going to kiss me. But, I want a real kiss." She shakes her head but smiles.

"Get to class, I'll give you a proper kiss after school. No need to get in more trouble." I pout. She has a point, but my next teacher is Mrs. Harden and she loves me. "Oh no. That pout won't work on me. Go. I'll see you in a little bit."

I give her a quick peck on the cheek. "If you insist."

"I do."

"See you in a few." I turn to walk to my class when I notice the rest of the guys are still staring. Lucian still hasn't moved, and we have the same next class. Lucian is never late. "Lucian, you ready? We have the same class, so we better get a move on before we're late."

"Y-yeah."

I smirk. It's nice to see Lucian stumbling around at a loss for words. You know, seeing as how he is always so good with them. I send Callie a wink before walking to my next class. It takes a moment, but Lucian follows and then speaks.

"What made you ask Callie out?"

"Why? You don't think I should have? I'm her mate too you know."

"I know. That's not how I meant it. I mean, what gave you the idea? None of us thought about it? I'm actually surprised none of us didn't think of it sooner."

I shrug my shoulders. "Honestly, I don't know. The only date she has been on was the group one to the bowling alley. We all know how well that worked out. Look, I know that I don't take things too seriously, I mean I do when necessary, but Callie needs a break from all of this. Hell, we need a break from all of this. I just thought what better way than to take her out and have some fun. Plus, we all need to spend time with her one on one. It's awesome doing things as a group, but we can't do everything together. Well, we could, though it might get awkward." I look over at Lucian and see his bewildered expression, and I can't help but to laugh. "I'm kidding, well mostly. It would probably be hella awkward, but I would do anything for Callie." Lucian shakes his head, but I see the smirk.

"It's a good idea Max, and your logic behind it is sound. You know you just opened a can of worms, right? The rest of are going to ask her out as well."

"I wouldn't expect anything less." I clap him on the back as we walk to our seats. Now, I need to plan for a date with my mate. Something fun. I know just the thing.

Graydon

I can't believe how stupid we've been. How the hell did none of us think to ask Callie on a date? We have to be some of the worst mates around. I wipe my hands down my face. Max out of all of us being the one who thinks of it first almost makes it worse. Though, it makes sense. He is what you would consider the ladies' man out of all of us. Before Callie arrived, I don't remember a time when he didn't have some date, or some girl lined up. I just hope that he doesn't treat Callie like she is just another notch in his belt, because if he does, I'll kick his ass. No way in hell would I let him or any of them treat Callie like crap.

I look over Callie's head to Zeke. He's frowning and seems lost in thought, and I would bet any money he's kicking himself in the ass about this whole thing as well. I cross my arms over my chest and scowl. I have no interest in doing whatever art project the teacher assigned up for the day. I glance at Callie, who is lost in her own thoughts. It's the smile on her face that catches my attention. I don't think I've seen a smile on her face like that since we met. Of course, Max is the one to put it there, Mr. Funny Guy. It only angers me more.

Why couldn't I have been the one to think of it? I could have had another one of Callie's first. Her first single date. Her first date was with all of us and I'm fine with that, but I also ruined it because of my attitude. Now I have to make it up to her when I ask her out on our date, because Max is crazy if he thinks no one else is going too. I just have to do it.

I clear my throat, but it comes out as more of a growl, which has Callie turning my way.

You okay?

Being able to silently communicate makes things a whole lot easier, especially in class.

Yes and no.

Care to explain.

I sigh. Here we go, my insecurities are coming out to play, and once again, I find myself telling her what's wrong.

I'm just kicking myself right now because of the whole date thing. I'm pissed that I didn't think to ask you out. I mean what kind of mate does that? I should know better.

Graydon, you're being too hard on yourself. I don't think any of us were even thinking about dates. We have a lot going on right now. We've all been so focused on trying to solve our war problems that things like dates have been put on the back burner.

I know you're right but still.

There will be plenty of time for dates once we defeat Circe and whoever she is helping.

I know, but Callie, I wait until she meets my eyes, *will you go out on a date with me sometime?*

She smiles, and I swear a piece of my black heart melts.

Of course, I would love to go out on a date with you.

The tightness in my chest eases. I didn't think she would say no. Callie is too good for me. She deserves someone better, but God help me, I couldn't stay away from her even if I tried. Even if we weren't mates, I would still have been drawn to her. I just don't know how well I could have broken through her barriers without the help of the others. I'm not exactly what you call warm and fuzzy.

The rest of Art passes by pretty quickly, and Zeke barely says a word. I was going to wait until after we walked Callie to next class before I talked to him, but I don't get the chance.

"Graydon, go on ahead. I'll make sure Callie gets to class. I need to talk to her anyway."

The corner of my mouth lifts slightly. I know what he's going to do, so I give him the privacy. I clap him on the shoulder before I walk away.

I don't understand why we are so nervous about this. It's not like we haven't all asked a girl out before. Out of all of us, I don't have the best luck with females. Now, I have to come up with a date to impress my mate. Where the hell am I going to take her? What the hell do we even have in common? Is it stupid to take her to do something that I like to do? Maybe she will end up enjoying it just as much as I do. Then it comes to me. I know exactly what we're going to do on our date, and the guys are going to kill me for it later, but it will so be worth it.

Zeke

Through Art class, all I could think about was how I was going to ask Callyn out. I shouldn't be this nervous. I think the last time I was this nervous to ask a girl out was the first time I did it. I didn't realize how long I was taking to ask her until I saw the gymnasium in front of me.

"Are you okay, Zeke? You've been acting weird since lunch."

Have I? I guess I've been quieter than normal, but I'm just wallowing in my own self-pity because I didn't think to ask Callie out on a date. One of the most fundamental things in a teenager's life and none of us, but Max, was smart enough to think of it.

I lift my hand and rub the back of my neck. "I'm okay. Um...I was just wondering if maybe...you would like to go out on a date with me?" I rush out. Then I start to look everywhere but at her.

"Zeke," her voice begging me to look at her. She smiles, and it's the best thing that I've seen. "I would love to go out on a date with you. Though you might want to talk to the others because all of you, but Lucian, has asked me out. We'll need to let everyone know what day their date is." She shakes her head. "I'm going to be a busy girl with the four of you, but I wouldn't have it any other way."

She steps forward and gives me a hug. I wrap my arms around her and bury my nose in her hair. I love the way she smells, like vanilla and strawberries. She pulls back and searches my face. I smile the biggest smile I can give because she has made me the happiest man alive.

"Go, before you're late for class. I have to hurry and change before I'm late as well."

I place a kiss on her forehead. "I'll see you in a little a bit." She nods before turning and walking into the girl's locker room. I turn and practically have to jog to make it to my next class. I just step into the room when the tardy bell rings.

I'm on cloud nine. She is going to be going on four dates, even if Lucian hasn't asked her yet, and I need to make sure I take her somewhere that the others won't think of. She likes to do new things mostly because she didn't get to experience a lot living with her stepdad. Maybe Callie is right, and we do need to have a talk, at least to figure out where everyone is taking her, so she doesn't go on a double date. It shouldn't be too hard to figure out.

I spend the rest of class trying to think of somewhere to take Callie. Class is almost over when I have an idea. I know where and what we're going to be doing on our date, and I can't wait.

Chapter 6

Callyn

No one can break my mood. Going out on dates with the guys wasn't something that crossed my mind. We're mates, and we kind of just fell into being together. There really hasn't been any opportunities to date. We always have something come up. First, it was my stepdad. I've never been more relieved than the day I found out we weren't really related. According to Aunt Dahlia, my real father died in an accident. I will never get the chance to know him. After that, it was the Elder Council and Kelsey Taylor who tried to kill me. Little did they know that would be all that was needed in order to get me to shift for the first time.

Shifting into a phoenix was all it took for some people to start following me, to believe that I am the next Alpha Queen. It also helped that I have four mates just like she did. Let's not forget the North Pack who tried to take out my mates. It didn't end well for some of them. Others fled, while some stayed behind. Those that have stayed have been loyal, so far. One of the things that Elder Harris, Lucian's grandfather, is doing is questioning them trying to find out any information that can give us some type of lead or idea about who and what their next move will be.

Cat had that vision and we are trying to figure out a way to stop that from coming true. Well, we have a plan; it's just putting it into motion. But in the midst of all the things that have been happening to me and my mates, going out on dates is the one thing we haven't thought about. I'm so excited. I can't wait to see what they plan for us to do. Each of them is so different, and I'm sure that their dates will reflect that. Lucian is the only one who hasn't asked me, but it's only a matter of time.

Max will probably plan something fun, Zeke...maybe something sporty. Lucian, I think will plan something intimate, something where it will just be the two of us. Now Graydon, he is a little tougher to pin down. He's more reserved than the others. I don't have any idea what we would do, but I can't wait to see what they come up with.

Gym has been pretty normal with Kelsey gone. Her entourage only makes comments to me when I pass by, which is fine with me. I can take that over them physically trying to get back at me, but it looks like Kelsey was their muscle. They lost their nerve without her here. I wonder if they are still in contact with her. I wouldn't be surprised if they are keeping her updated on me. There isn't much because me and the boys have been keeping to ourselves. We try not to talk about the war or anything pertaining to what is going on at school. Our trust circle is very small.

The chances that someone in town or even in school is working against us is high. You can never be too careful. My own thoughts carry me through the class and before I know it gym is over, and I'm sitting in my usual seat in study hall, between Graydon and Max.

In unusual style, Lucian is the last of us to arrive. Usually, it's me that is the last because of how far away the gym is. He doesn't say anything as he takes his seat. He fiddles around with his notebook. I just watch. It doesn't take long before he is ripping the page out and folding it. He turns, meets my eyes, and gives me a small smile before he hands the note to me. In true girly style, I giggle, but I take the note. I carefully open it, not wanting to rip it. There in his neat and tidy handwriting is him asking me out of a date.

Will you go out on a date with me?
Circle yes or no

Instead of circling the answer, because I want to keep the note, I answer him telepathically.

Yes Lucian. I would love to go out on a date with you. I give him the biggest smile I can muster, and I love the one he gives me back.

Excellent.

I can't wait to tell Cat. Plus, she can help me get ready. It's nice finally having a friend that I can talk to and depend on. Cat came into my life right when I needed her, and she has been proving her worth ever since.

"Guys, you have no idea how excited I am." I'm basically hopping up and down in my seat. I feel so hyper.

"We can tell. You're acting like Max," Graydon says.

I shrug my shoulders. "You're just gonna have to deal with me being this way. You're part of the reason for making me so happy in the first place."

He chuckles. "Well in that case, I'll let it slide."

You know he should really smile and laugh more. It transforms his face, and it's breathtaking. Not that he isn't gorgeous when he doesn't, it's just something about his smile.

"So, how are we doing this? Who and when am I going out with? Max has Friday night." I turn and look at him. "Is that this Friday night?"

"Yuppers. I already know where I'm taking you," He says with a grin.

"Who's next?"

"Seeing as how I asked you next, I think I should get the second date," Graydon states.

"That seems fair."

"Good. This Saturday afternoon and night."

I nod my head. I look between Lucian and Zeke.

"What I have planned can be done during the day," Lucian says.

"Mine is a night activity."

"I'll take Sunday morning and you Sunday night?"

"Sounds good to me."

"I can't wait."

This weekend is going to be the best.

Catori

I'm sitting in my last class when my phone buzzes in my pocket. I pull it out and see Callyn's name.

Callyn: Hey, I have a couple of things I want talk to you about.

Me: What's up?

Callyn: We have a plan to see where Alcina's loyalty lies. I want you to be there. You're good at reading people, and I want your take on her. I don't know. Maybe you can find a way to touch her and see if you can get anything from her. I would like to know now if she's going to betray us.

Me: Sounds good. When?

Callyn: I'm messaging her after school to see if she can do it tonight.

Me: What's your plan?

Callyn: Can you come over after school? I will explain it then.

I don't blame her for not wanting to send that message. If I were to leave or lose my phone, someone could see that message. People are shitty and would use that against her in a heartbeat. Damn shame, you can't trust anyone anymore.

Me: Yeah, I can.

Callyn: Cool. The other thing is all of the boys have asked me out on a date.

Callyn: Like one on one dates.

Took those boys long enough.

Me: About damn time.

Callyn: Right! But I can't blame them. With everything going on, we really don't have the time.

She has a point. Someone's been trying to kill her. When would they have found the time?

Me: I know, but you can't be stressing about this 24/7. You need time to relax and enjoy yourself.

Callyn: I know, but still. I was wondering if you wouldn't mind helping me get ready for the dates? I've never had a girl as a friend before, and I've never been on a date before. I can use all the help I can get.

Me: I'll help. When is the first date?

Callyn: Friday night with Max. Then Saturday with Graydon, Lucian is Sunday morning and Zeke Sunday night.

Me: Damn, they aren't waiting around. They're keeping you busy all weekend.

Callyn: I know. I'm excited yet nervous. These are my first dates. Ever.

Me: Well shit. We'll make sure they can't keep their eyes off of you.

Like that is going to be hard. One of them is always watching her. It's like they take turns. It's scary how good they are at it. I don't think there's a move she makes that one of them doesn't know about.

Callyn: Thank you. :)

Me: Anytime girl.

And I mean that. I know Callyn was testing me to see if my friendship was real, but I was doing the same to her. I couldn't let another Kelsey in my life. Not after everything she has done, but I knew I shouldn't have worried. I don't think Callyn has a bad bone in her body. Sure, she needs to toughen up and start standing up for herself but we're making progress. I've been helping her with that. Especially if she has any chance at defeating this mystery guy. She won't be doing it alone. I'll be there to help.

♛♛♛♛♛

"I texted Alcina, and she said she'll be here in an hour," Callyn says.

I just came straight to Callyn's after school. There was no point in going home knowing that I would have to come here anyways. She filled me on the plan and what she found out in the journal. It's a good plan, but I don't like that she will be giving Alcina that much information. Callie better hope this works, because I don't know if she can take another hit and come out on the other side.

You can sense when Alcina is going to appear. The air around you changes, feels heavier, for a brief moment. The next thing you know, she is standing before you. She's carrying a bag with her.

"Callyn, so good to hear from you. I wasn't sure after the way things went last time."

"Yeah, well we decided to give you chance to prove yourself. I found some interesting information in the journal. It talked of a talisman and how it was used to gather magic to make the user strong enough to defeat the Alpha Queen and her mates."

Good, she left out who it belonged to, giving her just the basics.

"What is it that you would like me to do?"

"I want to know if there is a way to locate the talisman?"

"Without something that belongs, like DNA, to the owner there is no way I can locate that."

"What If I told you that Circe was the witch who helped the person defeat the Alpha Queen, and that Circe is still alive."

Alcina starts to laugh, but when she realizes no one else is laughing with her, she stops.

"You're not kidding."

"No. Someone had a vision, and in that vision, Circe was alive and helping someone, or at least a descendant of hers with her namesake. Whoever she was helping had the talisman."

"A prophetess," Alcina whispers. "It truly is the age of a new Alpha Queen."

"Yeah, but we need a way to figure out who the mystery guy is and how to break the talisman or the spell on it, because let's just say it doesn't end well for us in that vision."

As Callyn has Alcina distracted I've moved closer to her. I'm almost standing behind her. I plan to just place my hand on her shoulder. I look at Callie, meeting her eyes, and motion for her to keep going.

"You said you need some form of DNA in order to find the person. Would a relative of that person work?"

"Essentially, yes. As long as the person is a blood relative."

I finish moving and place my hand on her shoulder. Alcina jumps.

"What are you doing?"

At first nothing happens. I'm just about to tell Callyn when my vision changes.

"Circe."

"Alcina, I presume. I've heard a lot about you through the grapevine. Powerful in your own right. This should be interesting. It's been a while since someone could take me on. Do you think you can?"

"I know I can."

Callyn and the boys stand up next to her. There is a maniacal laughter coming from behind Circe. A figure steps forward but not enough to reveal their face.

"You are no match for me. My talisman has been harnessing magic and power for over two hundred years. I will defeat you, just like my ancestor did to yours all those years ago. The only difference is I'm going to rule. I'm not going to make the same mistakes as he did."

"You're a descendant of Lorcan?" Callyn questions.

"Lorcan, the fool, was my great-great-great grandfather," he sneers. "The only thing he did right was make this talisman. Everyone that came after him was too weak and stupid to take control. But I'm not."

Circe makes the first move but Alcina counters it. The battle commences.

"You're the prophetess. You just had a vision, didn't you? What did you see?"

"You can trust her Callyn. I don't know the person's name, but I can tell you that the person who has the talisman is a descendant of Lorcan. I still couldn't see his face, but he admitted to the lineage."

"Lorcan has a descendant?" Alcina asks.

"Yes."

Callyn

"But that's not all," Cat states.

"Great, there's more? Of course, there is," Max states.

"This talisman," Cat continues, not fazed by Max, "he said it's been gathering magic and power over the last two hundred years."

"Shit," Graydon exclaims.

"Yeah. If we have any hope of defeating this guy, we need to take out that talisman. I don't think we can beat him any other way."

My eyes meet Alcina's. "We have a way of locating Lorcan's descendant. We have me, the descendant of the Alpha Queen. Do you have everything you need to do the spell?"

"Let me double check." Alcina pulls her bag over and starts to set items on the coffee table. "Everything is here." I watch as she starts to set up.

First, she lays down a map, next the cliché candles, a needle, and a silver chain. On the end of the chain is an almost translucent stone with a blue sheen. Alcina sees me looking intently at the stone. The way the light reflects off of it makes the sheen almost vary in shades of purples and greens, like a chameleon.

"It's a moonstone."

"It's beautiful."

"Moonstones are used for a variety of things and are very sought after. The purer the stone, the more power it will have. My little piece helps enhance any spell I cast. This should help us narrow down to a town."

"What do you need from me?"

"Just a few drops of your blood will do. I'll prick your finger and place a few drops of your blood in the center of the map. As I recite the spell, I'll move the moonstone necklace to the four cardinal points, north, south, east, and west. This will help move the blood across the map and stop at the city in which your relative is located." As she is explaining to me the spell process, she sets up and lights the candles. She places one at the top, bottom, and one on each side of the map.

"Does this take long?"

"No more than a few minutes." I nod. "Ready?"

I look at each of my guys and Cat. They all give me a slight nod of their head. They'll be here to help if something goes wrong or we turn out to be wrong about Alcina.

"Ready."

I move my hand over the map, palm up. Alcina runs the tip of the needle through the flame of a candle. Quickly, she pokes my finger and turns my hand. Gently she squeezes my finger until three drops of my blood hit the map. Alcina picks up the necklace and starts to sway it up, down, and side to side, over and over while mouthing the words to the spell. I watch the blood in rapt attention. It turns into a bubble and starts to slowly move over the map.

"Holy shit."

I look at Max. My thoughts exactly. I look back down not wanting to miss anything. It doesn't take long before the blood stops moving. All of us move closer to see. We're so close that one wrong move and we'll be bumping heads.

Riverwalk, Montana.

I gasp and move until my back hits the couch. Everyone is staring at me.

"Does Riverwalk mean something to you?"

"It's-it's the town I lived in before we came here."

"You mean to tell me that Lorcan's relative and his witch Circe, were in the same town?" Zeke questions.

"I don't know if we were there at the same time. I don't know what either of them look like."

"If they were in the same town as you, there is a chance they know who you are, even when you didn't. There would have been one reason for them to be there." We all look at Graydon. "To kill you."

"Either they didn't find you, or you left before they arrived," Alcina states.

"I'm lucky to be alive. I'm lucky that I even made it here to meet my mates."

"I'm going to call my grandfather and let him know what happened. Maybe he can send someone there and gather information."

All I can do is nod my head in agreement. People were out to kill me before I even knew who and what I am. The one good thing my stepfather has ever done for me was moving us around, town after town. Who knows what could or would have happened if we stayed any longer. I don't realize what is going on around me. I have no idea what anyone is talking about. I'm so consumed in my own thoughts that it takes Lucian bending down in front of me to snap me out of it.

"Hey, you okay?"

I shake my head. I'm on the verge of tears, and I'm trying so hard to hold them back, to be strong. I open my mouth to say something, but it feels like my throat is thick with emotion. I can't get a word out. Lucian must understand this because he starts talking to me telepathically.

Is it easier for you to talk to me this way?

Yes.

Are you okay?

No. I was just thinking about what could have happened if we didn't leave Riverwalk when we did.

Trust me, we all have the same thoughts running through our heads.

Then how come none of you seem bothered by this?

Because your here with us. Yes, it's scary to think about the what if's, but you can't do that. You're here with us in the here and now, and we couldn't be more grateful. You're only going to drive yourself crazy with those kinds of thoughts.

I know you're right, but it's hard not thinking them.

Lucian pulls me into his body, hugging me, and it's just what I need. I bury my nose in the crook of his neck, inhaling his warm cinnamon scent.

You're going to be okay, baby, I promise. We won't let anything happen to you. Everything happens for a reason. You leaving Riverwalk and coming here. You were meant to be here...with us.

He's right. I know he is, but it's going to take me a little bit before I can let it go.

"Come, baby, I messaged my grandfather and I want to tell everyone what he said." He lets me go but just long enough, so he can sit on the couch by me. He reaches over and laces our fingers together. "Guys." Everyone stops and looks at Lucian. "I heard back from my grandfather and he is going to send someone to Riverwalk to see if they can find Circe and whoever she is helping, or at the very least, information on them."

"Good. Hopefully it won't take too long."

"I know you're impatient Graydon, but something like this, something that could be this valuable, I want the information to be correct."

"This is going to change everything. Every plan, every strategy, everything we do from now on can be used to take this guy out," Zeke states.

"Exactly."

"You mean for once, we might have the upper hand? Hell yea."

I smile and shake my head. Maybe Max is right. Maybe we can get the upper hand and that can change the tide in our favor. I need this. I need to finally be a step ahead of everyone who has been trying to kill me. I need to stop them once and for all.

Callyn

It's been a week, and the only word we have gotten so far is that the person Elder Harris has sent to Riverwalk has arrived. I'm hoping that in the next couple of days we'll have more information. But instead of thinking about that, I'm waiting on Cat to get here so she can help me get ready for my first date.

To say that I'm excited is an understatement. I've had the biggest, goofiest smile on my face all day. School seemed to drag on and on. I used to be grateful for days like that, but today, I just wanted the day to be over. I get to go on four dates over the next three days. I get to spend quality time with all my mates. There is a knock on my bedroom door before it opens.

"Cat," I say excitedly.

"Callie. Are you ready for this?"

"Yes. This is my first real date, well I mean individually."

"Who are you going out with?"

"Max."

"Did he say where he is taking you?"

"No."

"Since it's Max, I'm going to suggest that you wear pants because you never know what he's got up his sleeve. You can count on it being fun."

"Do you have any idea what it could be?"

"I honestly couldn't tell you what he has planned. Knowing Max, it could be anything."

I nod my head in agreement. "Okay, so pants it is."

"Do you mind if I go through your closet?"

"Like you have to ask."

I watch as Cat opens the door to my closet and slowly starts shifting through the items. I notice Cat has been more pensive lately. Maybe asking her to do this with me was a mistake. I don't want to feel like I'm rubbing my mates in her face. What kind of friend does that make me? Then again, she's the new prophetess, and I haven't asked her how she's been dealing with this.

"Hey Cat, are you okay?"

Cat turns to look at me. "Yeah, why do you ask?"

"I don't know. You don't seem like yourself, more reserved than usual." She shrugs her shoulders. Now I know something is up. Cat is always the first to tell you how it is, never one to hold back her thoughts. It's one of the things that I value the most about her. I can trust her not to sugar coat things with me. I guess I need to do that with her. "Cat tell me what's wrong. You can't tell me there isn't something wrong. If you don't start talking, I'll force it out of you. I'm trying to be the friend that you are to me. So, spill." She sighs and relents. Cat walks over and sits next to me on my bed.

"Being a prophetess is a lot of responsibility. Don't get me wrong, I'm thankful it's me now and not Kelsey. But seeing your death and not knowing what to do to stop it is getting to me. I want to make sure that vision doesn't come true."

"I'm stressing about it too, but I'm trying to take Lucian's advice and focus on the here and now. That's all we can do. I honestly thought that the reason you were so gloomy was because of the date thing. You know I don't want to rub my mates in your face, and if this is too much, please let me know. I don't want to hurt you."

"I'm fine about this. Trust me, I'd tell ya. I know one day I'll meet someone." She bumps her shoulder into mine. "Come on, let's get you ready for your date."

"You sure you're okay?"

"I will be. I'm going to take Lucian's advice. We'll figure out a way to stop that vision from coming true."

Cat gets up and walks back to my closet and starts to rifle through my things. She's trying to put on an act, trying to placate me, but I can tell she's still thinking about it. She turns with a hanger in her hands.

"Do you have black jeans?" I nod my head. "Good, wear those and this." She hands me a nude pink, half-sleeved shirt with purplish, pink roses on it. There are ties at the elbow and the shirt can be wore off the shoulder. She bends down and starts to go through my shoes. “These will be prefect.” She adds my flat, nude sandals with flowers that go from between the toe up to the ankle. There is a single strap around the heel. “Now all that is left is your hair. Go change, and I’ll do your hair and makeup next.”

I gather the items and move to my bedroom door. Before I leave, I glance back. Cat isn’t fooling anyone. I need to make sure I fix this. I can’t have my best friend feeling like it all rests on her. I’m going to make sure we change that vision. I need my Cat back.

Maximus

I run my hands through my hair. I’ve taken other girls out on a date, but this is different, this is my mate. I take a deep breath before I get out of my car. I look at myself in the side mirror, fixing my hair. I square my shoulders and walk up to the front door. I ring the doorbell, Callie’s aunt answers.

“Come on in.” Aunt Dahlia moves to the base of the steps. “Callie, Max is here,” she yells. “Give her a minute, and she’ll be down.” She gives my shoulder a squeeze before she walks away and into the living room.

I stay where I’m at. I don’t want to miss that first sight of her. I run my hands through my hair and start to pace. I don’t know why I’m so nervous. Someone clearing their throat catches my attention. I look to the top of the stairs and she’s beautiful. I’m one of the luckiest guys in the world. I can’t help the whistle that escapes my lips.

“Damn, girl.”

Callie giggles and shakes her head. What? Like she should have expected something else. She looks beautiful all the time, but dressed up, with a little bit of makeup, and that smile...she’s breathtaking. She walks down the stairs and stands in front of me.

“You look good Max.”

“You look hot; I mean you look gorgeous.” She rolls her eyes.

“So, where are we going?”

“Nope, I’m not saying. It’s a surprise.” Callie walks to the living room, picking up a jacket from the back of the couch.

"We're heading out, what's my curfew?"

"Be back by midnight. But before you go, I want a picture."

"Aunt Dahlia, really," Callie whines.

"Yes. Come on Max." I step next to Callie placing an arm around her waist. We wait for her aunt to grab her phone. "Smile." We do. "One more." I wait until the last second and place a kiss on Callie cheek. "Perfect."

"Come on, angel; let's go." I take her hand and lead her outside. I open the door and help her get in my car. I jog around to the driver side. "Ready to have some fun?"

"Of course." I smile.

I drive us to the next town over. I'm taking Callie on another first, well at least I hope so. I pull into the parking lot, glancing at her every so often so I can see her expression.

"Skating? You're taking me skating?"

"Yup." Callie lets out a squeal before leaning over the console, placing a kiss on my cheek.

"Thank you, thank you, thank you. I haven't been skating before. I'm so excited."

She's literally bouncing in her seat. I smile. This is a moment that I'll remember. The look on her face, the smile, the light in her eyes. I get out of the car, jogging to her side, so I can open the door for her. I hold out my hand; she places hers in mine.

"Let's go skating."

♛♛♛♛♛

"Max!" Callie practically screams as she wobbles like a newborn deer. I take hold of her hands, making sure she stays upright.

"I've got you. Now, slow...glide, don't try and walk normally. Gently push yourself forward."

"That's easy for you say, you're freaking skating backwards," she hisses.

"You'll learn. The more you do it, the easier it will become."

"I think I need a break. We've been at it for an hour, and I'm not any better from when we started."

"I'll let you take a break on one condition." She raises her eyebrow. "I get a kiss first." I smile as she rolls her eyes, but I see the smirk on her lips.

"Ugh. You know you're asking for a lot. I mean that quite literally. I can't even stand on my own two feet at the moment."

"I'll take my chances."

Holding her hands, I use the fact that she's on skates to my advantage. I pull her forward; her feet gliding over the slick roller rink floor. Since Callie doesn't know how to stop, she rolls right into my body. I grab her around her waist, keeping her steady.

"You planned this didn't you?"

"Nooooo, but I'll take every chance I get to get my hands on you," I say right before pressing my lips to hers.

The one thing I never get tired of is feeling her in my arms, her scent, her touch, her taste. She sighs and relaxes against me. I use my tongue to run along the seam of her lips, getting her to open them, her tongue meeting mine. I'm so wrapped up in Callie that I don't hear the lady at first. It takes for her to tap me on my shoulder before I listen.

"You might want to take that somewhere else. There are children here," she says with a huff.

Callie is so startled that she tries to back away from me, forgetting that she is on skates. She starts to lose her balance. Callie's feet start to slide out from underneath her. She reaches for me and in the process her skates get tangled up with mine, and the next thing I know, we're both falling. I know I can't stop us, but I grab onto her arms at the last second pulling her toward me. We land in a tangle of limbs with Callie on top of me. She pushes back slightly and looks down at me.

"Well, this isn't exactly what I had in mind for the first time I got you on top of me." I give her a wink. She just stares at me, her mouth forming an o. Something clicks, and she scrambles to get up but failing. "Geez, I'm not going to take how fast you're trying to get away from me personally."

I get up, holding out my hands to help Callie. She takes them.

"I'm sorry, I didn't mean..." I hold up a hand stopping her.

"It's not your fault. I just forget where I'm at when I'm with you. Besides, the lady had a point. If we continued any further, it probably would have gotten indecent, and then I would have had to try to explain why we got in trouble to Graydon, your aunt, and my parents and none of us want that."

She sighs, "I know but that still doesn't make me feel any better. I fell on you."

"Oh no, that is the highlight of my night so far. Come on, I think we've both had enough of this." She nods her head. I help her off the floor and to a nearby table. "I'll go get our shoes."

I'm just about to go when the cha cha slide starts playing. I look at Callie and smirk. I make my way back out on the floor. I go through the motions for doing the moves for the dance, making a production of it for Callie. It seems to be working because every time I look at her, she's smiling or laughing. Every time the song says criss-cross, I turn and skate backwards and cross my legs. Leaving the floor before the song is over, I skate back to Callie, stopping in front of her.

"Show off." I smile and give her a quick kiss before going to get our shoes from where we left them.

Callyn

I've never been skating, and honestly, I don't think I want to again. It's harder than it looks, and I'm so embarrassed. I can't believe we were making out in a room full of people, not just any people. Oh no. It's a room full of kids. I groan and bury my face in my hands. I can't say I'm sorry that the kiss happened, because I'm not. It was hot, and I want a repeat, just when it's more private. Then when you think it couldn't get worse, it does. I fell on him. Again, I can't say that I'm mad about it, it just could have been better timing.

I loved being pressed up against his body. He thinks embarrassment had me moving off of him, but it wasn't. No, I could feel his excitement. His body giving him away on just how happy he was to have me on him. I was just as happy, but I moved because I didn't trust myself not to touch him more intimately. Like I said, could have been better timing. These boys are going to be the death of me.

I don't notice Max coming back; it takes him moving my hands from my face.

"You okay, angel?"

"Yeah."

"Are you sure? There is nothing for you to be ashamed of. Also, you should know by now that you don't have to throw yourself at me like that. I'm a willing participant in anything you want to do."

I look into his cerulean blue eyes. There's a twinkle in them, making them shine. I love the mischief that seems to always be in them. I don't stop myself from grabbing him around his neck and pulling him towards me, placing my lips on his. I make sure not to get too carried away this time. I pull back after a few seconds.

Max clears this throat. "Do you want to go and get ice cream?"

"Sure."

It doesn't take us long to change out our shoes, grab our jacket, and be on our way to the ice cream shop.

We're waiting in line, browsing the menu, when it happens.

"Do you know what you want?"

"Smores." I answer when something catches my attention out of the eye. "Holy shit."

"What, what's wrong?" I can't say anything, so I point to the door. "Holy shit." Exactly.

We're both stunned into silence. We haven't seen or heard a peep from her since everything went down. I can't take my eyes off of the door. I'm just waiting to see what she's going to do when she sees us standing here. It doesn't take long since Max and I are standing in line a few feet from the door. You can't miss us. Her expression is everything I thought it would be.

Shock is the first thing that registers across her face, then comes the anger. I'm waiting for her to make a scene, to say or do something, but she does nothing. Instead, she turns around and walks right back out the door. I turn and look at Max the same time he turns to look at me. I can read his thoughts clear on his face because they are the same as mine. This can't be good. In no universe is having her come back a good thing, but Kelsey-fucking-Taylor just walked back into our lives.

Chapter 8

Graydon

Callyn and Max filled us in on Kelsey returning, but we all agreed to wait until Monday to figure out how to deal with it. This weekend is supposed to be relaxing, a way for all of us to have one on one time with her, and I'll be damned if I let Kelsey returning take away from that. I'm just going to be more vigilant, not like I wouldn't be with Callie anyways. I'm not going to risk or lose my mate because I decided to slack off and think that we're safe. D.T.A. Don't trust anyone, words to live by. If our lives over the last few months haven't been a clue to that, I don't know what will.

I arrived at Callie's earlier than I planned, but I needed to see her, to hear her, to make sure she was unharmed. It's not that I don't trust Max to keep her safe, because I know he will. I know he would lay his life on the line to save her, but I wasn't there, and I just needed to be sure. Callie didn't seem to mind. We passed the time by watching a movie and her asking me questions, which surprisingly I answered without giving her grief. Maybe the guys are right and she's making me soft, well when we're alone. I'll still beat the shit out of anyone who dares harm her.

I'm waiting in the living room for Callie to come back. She went upstairs to change. I told her to wear long sleeves, jeans, and sneakers. I have one of my old leather jackets in my truck for her to wear when we get there. I also need to make sure she doesn't look in the bed of the truck either, because that has the surprise to the second part of our date. I can't wait to see her face for the first part. I made sure I didn't tell the guys what we were doing because I know they wouldn't approve.

They would think that I was putting her in danger. I scoff at the idea, like I would purposefully do that. Though I can't wait to see what she looks like on the back of a motorcycle. Hell, I can't wait to have her arms wrapped around me, pressing her body against mine. I growl at the thought.

"You okay, Graydon?" I turn at the sound of Callie's voice.

I can't even form words. Her clothes aren't fancy, more plain and simple, but she makes them look extraordinary. She's wearing blue jeans, and a burgundy, plaid, long-sleeved shirt. But the thing that pulls me in is the low ponytail. She hardly wears her hair up, but when she does...man. That's when I notice she is looking at me with a frown on her face. Shit, she asked me a question and I haven't answered her, but she can't blame me. Whenever she's near, I can't focus on anything but her.

"I'm fine. I was just thinking."

"What are you thinking about?" she asks as she walks closer to me.

"Our date."

"Oh, and where are we going on our date?"

"I can't tell you; it's a surprise."

"You know Max said the same thing yesterday. I hate and love surprises at the same time." I can't relate to that because I hate surprises. "I just need to tell my aunt we're going. I'm warning you now, she's going to want to take pictures. She did last night."

I watch as she walks to the kitchen, admiring the sway of her hips. Which serves to distract me until she is out of view. Wait, did she say pictures? Aw hell.

♛♛♛♛♛

Callie wasn't kidding when she said her aunt would want to take pictures. I only did for Callie. I would do anything for her, even getting my picture taken. After what seemed like a million pictures, I walked Callie out to my truck. I had to make sure I blocked her view of the bed because I have pillows, blankets, and a cooler in the back. Once she was seated, I made my way over to the other side and got in. It wasn't long before we were heading over to the next town, to the motorcycle shop I sometimes worked at.

Lucky for me, the owner is a shifter; otherwise, I probably wouldn't have been allowed to work in the shop, at least not when I was underage. I had to have a conversation with him as well about what is happening. Not that he wouldn't have known about it anyways. Things tend to travel fast in the shifter community. He is giving me time to get this handled, and he'll hold my job for me. Though, while I'm here I should ask if he would be willing to stand and fight with us. He's a fellow bear shifter, and we can use all the power we can get.

I glance at Callie and wonder how she's going to take being on a motorcycle. We're about to find out because we're pulling into the drive. Her eyes widen.

"What are we doing here?"

"I'm taking you for a ride."

"A ride? On a motorcycle?"

"Yup."

"Will they let you do that?"

"I work here on occasion. They know they can trust me. The question is do you trust me to take you for a ride?"

"Absolutely." I smile, a real smile.

"Good, then let's get to it."

I get out and move over to Callie to help her get down. I don't have runners on the side of my truck and because Callie is short she has to turn to the side and hop down. Why would I let her do that, when I can help her down and have another reason to put my hands on her. I'm getting as bad as the others. Always needing to be near and touching her. I know I'm worse in some ways, like wanting to be her first for everything. I know that's not possible, and I shouldn't get angry or jealous, but I can't help it. It's who I am.

I open the shop door for her, gesturing for her to go in ahead of me. There's a jingle from the bell above the door when I close it behind me. It doesn't take long before Mr. Ferguson comes out from the back.

"Well, look at what the bear dragged in." I move around Callie and shake Mr. Ferguson's hand. "And who is this lovely lady?"

"This is Callyn Silvers, my mate."

"Well, I'll be damned," he says in a whisper.

Next thing I know he's kneeling on one knee, head bowed in front of Callie. She looks to me then back down to the old man before her.

What do I do?

I don't know. I've never seen someone do that before.

Is there a protocol I have to follow?

Lucian would know. I have no idea what to do.

Well, I have to do something?

"You don't have to do that, sir."

"You're the Alpha Queen. I'm showing my respect."

"Thank you, Mr. Ferguson. You may rise now."

"Should you need anything, please don't hesitate to ask." Callie nods her head. Well that saves me from having to ask him if he would help out.

"Thank you." Then the old man does something in the few years that I've known I never seen... he smiles.

"Now, what can I do for you today?"

"I would like to take Callie out for a ride."

Callyn

I didn't know what to do when Mr. Ferguson knelt before me. When the boys did it, after the barn fire, it was natural instinct. But this is something else. I don't think I did too bad. He seems to be happy, but judging by the look on Graydon's face, this doesn't seem like a normal reaction from this man. Is this going to be the new normal? I don't want people thinking that just because I'm going to be the new Alpha Queen that they are below me, because they're not. I don't want people kneeling before me. I want them to be comfortable. I want them to be able to come up to me with their issues and not fear what I'm going to do or how they should act. That's not the type of ruler I want to be.

Movement from the corner of my eye catches my attention. A few of the other workers have come from the back. I move closer to Graydon. One, because I don't know any of them and two, as Graydon would say D.T.A. We don't know who is on our side and who's not. Just because Graydon knows these guys doesn't mean that they can be trusted. I don't like how they are watching, staring. They openly leer at me; not giving a damn. Half of them have a sneer on their face, looking at me with disgust. The other half looks like the want to grovel at my feet, swear their allegiance. Graydon must since my unease because he grabs my hand and pulls me into his side, the one away from the prying eyes.

You okay?

I don't like how they keep looking at us. I'm not sure they are on our side, Graydon.

You feel it too?

Yes.

Then let's get the bike and get out of here before something happens.

"So, I'm going to let you take the Dyna Glide," Mr. Ferguson says as he leads us over to the row of bikes.

He stops in front of a matte black, chrome, two-seater. I walk forward, without touching the bike, I glide my hand along its body. This bike is beautiful.

"I take it she likes it. Man, you're one lucky kid." I love the smile that crosses Graydon's face.

"Thank you, Mr. Ferguson, for this," I say.

"No trouble at all. Best get going."

Graydon swings his leg over the bike, releasing the kickstand. He walks the bike over the garage style door. Mr. Ferguson hits a button from somewhere over by the front desk and the door rises. Graydon continues to walk the bike until we are back outside. The garage door closes behind us. Graydon puts the kickstand back down. I can't help looking at his butt in his jeans. I bite my lip and openly ogle him. I want nothing more than to go over there and smack his ass. We walk back to his truck, opening the back door, pulling out two helmets and a leather jacket. I eye him up and down, the boy is gorgeous. He has on a black, Henley t-shirt, jeans, leather jacket, and black, motorcycle boots. The sides of his hair are due for a trim, and the his longer black hair on top is slicked back.

"See something you like?" he asks as he walks back toward me. His mossy, green eyes sparkle with a hint of knowing and mischief.

"You know I do."

"Good." He places both of the helmets on the bike seats before opening the leather jacket. "This was mine from a few years ago. It might be big, but it will keep the cold out."

I take the couple of steps that separate us, presenting my back so he can help me put the jacket on. Graydon was right, I feel warmer already. Though I don't know if that heat is from the jacket or from him. He moves my hair, places an arm around my waist pulling me closer to him. I feel his warm lips on my neck. My hands move to his arm that is wrapped around me. I move my head to the side giving him better access. He continues to kiss my neck making his way up to my ear. His teeth nip at my earlobe. I moan.

"We should get going before I don't stop," he whispers in my ear.

I know he's right, but I don't want him to stop.

Graydon

I wanted to keep going, but this is not the time or the place. We have to get going so we can get to the second part of this date. Reluctantly, I release her and take a step back from her. I walk over to the bike, adjusting myself as I go. Grabbing both helmets, I turn and hand her one. I watch as she puts on the helmet, but before she can buckle the strap, I do it for her. She's looks cute, and I can't resist giving her a quick kiss before lowering the chin guard.

I have to give her credit. These new helmets are quite heavy, especially to someone who is not use to wearing them, but so far, so good. I grab my helmet, put it on, swing my leg over the bike, and release the kickstand. I hold my hand out for Callie and help her on. Seeing Callie on the back of a bike has got to be the sexiest thing I've ever seen. I'm glad I get this moment to myself.

Don't wiggle around and wrap your arms around my waist. Hold on tight.

I start the bike and head toward the road. A few turns and I can really open up on the road. Callie's grip on me tightens the faster I go. We're on the road, on the outskirts of town, weaving our way alongside the lake, when her grip finally loosens. I can feel her relax.

This is amazing. I understand why you enjoy this. Thank you for sharing this with me.

Anytime, Callie bear.

♛♛♛♛♛

We make it back to the shop right before closing. Lucky for us, none of the guys are here from earlier. I dropped the bike off and thanked Mr. Ferguson again. I swear all Callie had to do was smile at the old man and he was putty in her hands. I help Callie into my truck and take a slow walk all the way around. With the bad feeling we both had earlier, I had to check my truck to make sure no one messed with it. I doubted they would with Mr. Ferguson here, but people are stupid and have been known for doing crazy things.

Plus, I doubt any of them would want to take me on. See most people don't know of our extra abilities, affinities with the elements. We've been practicing and have gotten pretty good at controlling them on our own, but nothing beats when Callie is touching us, helping us. Through the training, we have realized she has a little magic of her own. She doesn't have the ability to channel one of the elements. Her powers are subtler. It only seems to appear when she is helping one us channel and control our powers.

"Thank you for taking me for a ride. I've never felt freer. It was incredible." You can tell by the look on her face that she means it.

"Well, we're not done yet."

There's a field not far from where we live that I'm taking her to. There are no street lights, no houses, no cars, no noise. By the time that we get there, it will just be getting dark enough for what I have planned.

"Where are we going? You know the motorcycle ride was enough."

"I know, but I wanted to show you that there is more to me than the grumpy person you see every day."

"But I love the grumpy person you are, if you weren't you wouldn't be my grumpy bear. I don't want you to change who you are. I love you exactly as you are."

"I know that, but I still want to show you I can be romantic too."

"You are in ways that you don't even realize."

I was going to ask her what she meant, but we were coming up to the spot that I wanted to take her.

"Now, I need you to close your eyes. I have a few things that I need to get ready before you can get out. No peeking," I say as I put the truck in park.

"I promise, no peeking." She closes her eyes, covering them with her hands for good measure.

I hop out of the truck and go to the bed, lowering the tailgate. I climb up, making quick work of the pillows and blankets.

"Are you almost done?"

"Getting impatient, are we?"

"Yes," she drags out.

"Good thing ..." I hop off the side, opening her door, "...that I'm done then." I place my hands on her waist and help her down. "Keep your eyes closed just a little bit longer." I guide her to the bed of the truck. "Okay, you can open them." She looks at the bed and then back to me. "We're stargazing tonight."

Callyn

Graydon has gone above and beyond tonight. I wasn't lying when I said the bike ride would have been enough, but now that I've seen the bed of the truck, no way am I passing up the opportunity to cuddle with my grumpy bear. And as much as I love his grumpiness, I love seeing this softer side to him too.

He helps me up, and I snuggle down in the blankets. Graydon doesn't waste any time before he is cuddling up next to me. For a while, neither of us say a word, just content on looking at the night sky.

"What did you mean when you said I'm romantic in ways that I don't realize?"

"It's the little things you do, holding my hand, helping me in and out of your truck. The way you're protective of me, the way you can't seem not to touch me when we are near. They may not seem like much to you, but to me they are everything."

He pulls me closer to his body, tilting my head. "I love you, Callyn."

"I love you too, Graydon."

He gives me the sweetest kiss. This is one of the best moments of my life.

Callyn

The last two days have been amazing. Max and Graydon both gave me memories that I will never forget. I love the time I got to spend with them. Here I sit, anxious to go on my date with Lucian. My strong and silent type. He doesn't say much but when he does everyone listens. I'm excited to see what he has planned for us. I do have to say, I was a little surprised that Graydon took me stargazing. I thought for sure that Lucian would have been the one to do that, explaining the constellations, pointing them out.

Spending that quiet time with Graydon was prefect. I've been trying to guess all morning what Lucian and I could be doing, and I'm drawing a blank. Whatever it is, I know it will definitely be all Lucian.

There is a knock at the door. I go to answer it, but my aunt beats me there. One thing I never get tired of is seeing my guys. Every time they walk into a room or are just standing nearby, I realize how lucky I am to have them in my life. I thank whatever forces brought me to them.

"Are you ready to go Callie?"

"Yup."

"Wait," my aunt says. "I need to get pictures first." I groan. "Oh, come on, it's just a few."

"She's lying. She takes like twenty," I stage whisper.

"Well, the faster you get over here the faster it will be done."

"She has a point," Lucian says.

"Fine." We take the required photos, and then we're on our way. "So, are you going to tell me what we're doing?"

"Nope." It doesn't take long before we are pulling up to a park. I look at Lucian, raising one of my eyebrows. "I have a plan. Trust me."

"I do." We park, and Lucian helps me out of his car. He goes to the trunk and pulls out a picnic basket. "We're going on a picnic?"

"Yep."

I squeal, throwing my arms around his neck, hugging him tight. "Thank you."

He grabs my hand and we walk over to one of the pavilions. Lucian places the basket on the bench, digging through it, grabbing a table cloth and placing it on the table. He then goes and sets everything up. It's such a simple display of sandwiches, chips, and fruit, but it's one of the sweetest gestures.

"I know it's not much but..." he trails off.

"This is absolutely perfect."

Lucian

It's always easy to forget that Callyn hasn't done a lot of things, being sheltered and kept hidden. The simple things in life make her happy. I hope we can all keep doing that, keep the smile that is on her face right now there. I wasn't sure how she was going to take this date. Max and Graydon told us what they did afterward, and let's just say that we weren't happy with Graydon. He should have never taken her for a ride on a motorcycle. He put her safety in jeopardy.

"Hey, you okay?" I didn't realize I zoned out.

"Yeah, I'm okay. Just thinking."

"What were you thinking about? Maybe I can help."

"It's nothing important." She puts her sandwich down.

"Clearly it is if it's drawing your attention away."

"It's just me being over protective."

"How so?"

I sigh. "I was just thinking of how dangerous it was for Graydon to take you out on that ride."

"Why?"

"Motorcycles are too open, there is nothing to protect you if you get in an accident."

"We both wore helmets, he didn't do anything crazy with me on the back. Honestly, who better to take me for a ride than Graydon? He loves motorcycles, and you should know he would never risk my life. Graydon could get hurt just as easily."

She has a point. I'm so focused on what I can to do to protect her that I haven't thought about the rest of us. One way to hurt Callie would be if one of us was killed or hurt.

"You're right."

"Damn straight, and don't you forget it." She smiles before she starts to laugh which causes me to laugh.

"You should really laugh and talk more. I love the sound of your voice." I look away.

"I always felt like you shouldn't say something unless it was important. There was no point for idle chit-chat for me. Max talks enough for the rest of us."

"Well, that last part is true." She chuckles. "I wouldn't care what you wanted to talk about, just as long as you did." Callie reached across the table, grabbing my hand, giving it a gentle squeeze.

"Maybe I will do that, but only with you."

"I'd like that."

"Let's get this packed up." In silence, we worked together to clear off the picnic table. I grabbed the basket, jogging back to my car, placing it in the trunk. Callie was headed my way before I held up my hands in a stop gesture. "Wait," I said when I got close enough. I grab her hand, pulling toward the swings. "Sit." She obeys. I stand behind her, putting my hand in the center of her back, giving her a slight push.

"I haven't swung on a swing since I was a little girl." I figured as much. "You know, I always felt like I was flying."

"And now."

"I still do but in a different way."

"What way is that?" I ask as I stop her by gripping the chains. She tilts her head back meeting my gaze.

"The heart pounding, pulse racing, kind of flying," she whispers.

I move my hand to her neck, holding her in place. I watch as her pupils dilate. Slowly, I lower my head; my eyes never leaving hers. My lips press onto hers, gently at first, but then more brutally. I softly squeeze her neck. The sound of her moan almost undoes me. We kiss a little longer before I pull away, releasing her. Both of us are breathing hard. This girl tests all my control. It takes a minute before either of us can speak. I'm lucky that her back is to me, so she doesn't see just how much she affects me.

I clear my throat. "We should get going. I have one more place I want to take you before I have to get you back for your date with Zeke." She simply nods her head. I can't help the smirk that comes across my face. If this leaves her speechless, just you wait.

Callyn

Lucian's other surprise was a trip to the bookstore. I could have spent hours in there, but we only stayed an hour. He ended up getting a couple of his favorite books for me. I can't wait to read them, so we can talk. Oh, we can have a two-person book club. The best part about the trip was seeing Lucian come alive. The boy loves his books. He was practically dragging me around the store. I didn't mind one bit. It was awesome seeing him so open, seeing his eyes light up. It was the best. That kiss...that kiss on the swing was something else. His kisses are like nothing else. The urge to submit to him is strong. I don't feel that way with the others. There is a power lurking behind the quiet demeanor of his. I can't wait to help unleash it.

I look at my phone and jump out of bed. I have less than thirty minutes to get ready for my date with Zeke. I grab a pair of jeans, a plain gray t-shirt, and my favorite black boots. I get dressed as fast as I can. I'm in the middle of brushing my hair when my aunt calls me.

"Callie, Zeke is here." I quickly finish, putting my hair up in a ponytail. I swipe some Chapstick on my lips and head to the stairs.

There, standing at the bottom with a bouquet of flowers, is Zeke. His amazing gold eyes staring up at me with a smile on his face. I race down the stairs and throw myself at him. He stumbles but catches his footing, wrapping his arms around me. I don't think, I just act, and I place my lips to his. I realize how much I missed him. I kept kissing him until I heard the click of a camera. I turn my head and see my aunt taking pictures.

"Aunt Dahlia," I exclaim. "Could you have waited?"

"No. It was a perfect moment. Wait until you see the pictures. You'll see what I'm talking about. Now, go and have fun."

Zeke waits until my aunt leaves before he places me on my feet. He takes a step back and presents me with the flowers.

"Thank you," I say as I take them. I bring the flowers to nose, taking a deep breath. "They smell so good."

"I'm glad you like them."

"I love them. Let's put them in water before we go." He follows me to the kitchen, watching me as I put the flowers in a vase. "So, are you going to tell me what we're doing?"

"Nope." I shake my head.

"I just need to grab a jacket and we can get going."

I grab the leather jacket I left on the back of the kitchen table chair. Zeke takes it and helps me into it. Grabbing my hand, he leads me the front door and out to his SUV, opening the passenger door. I get in and he closes it, walking to the driver side.

"Are you ready to have some fun?" he asks as he starts the vehicle and heads to our destination.

"Of course."

"Good. I know we said this weekend we weren't going to talk about the war or anything related to that, and I'm going to keep to that, but I just want to say Elder Harris has some information for us."

"I hope that it's good news because we can use more of that now."

"I agree, but for tonight, it's just me and you." I look over at Zeke and smile.

"I can't wait to see what you have planned. All you have been so amazing, and I've gotten to do a lot of things that I've never done before."

"Well, the one thing that I can tell you is that you will be doing another first."

"Oh, now I need to know. You can't say something like that and not tell me."

Zeke shakes his head. "Not going to happen, sweetheart."

"Ugh. All of you are impossible."

"We all love the look on your face and the excitement in your eyes when you get do something new."

"I must have that look all the time then, since I didn't get to do much."

"Yeah, but that gives us the privilege of getting to experience it with you."

I turn to look out the window. My life was hard before I met the guys, but it has changed so much since then that it's almost hard to believe. I hate thinking about it, and for the most part, I don't but sometimes, like now, it pops up.

"Hey, you okay?"

"Yeah, just thinking about how much my life has changed. I don't know how I would have survived if I didn't meet you and the others."

"Lucky, for us."

More like lucky for me. I stare out the window, watching the now familiar scenery go by as we head out of town. The rest of the car ride is silent, but it doesn't take us long to get where we're going. We pull up to a Go-Kart and mini golf course.

"Oh. My. God." I start bouncing in my seat.

"I take it that you like it."

"This is awesome!"

"Once the weather warms up some more, they'll open the outside course, but the inside one is where all the fun is at. Just you wait."

Zeke

Callie has no idea what awaits her inside. She's so excited that she doesn't even wait for me to open her door. Instead, I see her waiting outside my door.

"Come on slowpoke." Her excitement is infectious. I quickly get out of the car, grabbing her hand and leading her inside.

"Holy. Shit."

Everything is neon colors. There are black lights and strobe lights everywhere. The place is divided into three sections, go-kart, mini golf, and paintball. There is a small area off to the side of the paintball where they house the paint drum. We're going to do everything. I figured we start with the mini golf, then the go-kart, paintball, then finally the paint drum. That has to be my favorite part of the whole thing.

"Okay, so which are we doing?"

"Don't you mean which are we doing first?"

"Wait, we're doing more than one?"

"We're doing all of them." She squeals, jumping into my arms.

"Thank you, thank you, thank you." Callie places a kiss on my cheek. "So, which are we doing first?"

"Mini golf."

"Then lead the way."

We get in line, I pay for the round of golf, and we pick our ball color. It takes her a couple of holes before she starts to get the hang of it, but I ended up winning. Callie takes it graciously. I don't even think she cares if she wins, she's just having fun.

"Can we go on the go-karts next?"

"Anything you want."

"Yay!" She grabs my arm and drags me over. "This may be the *one* thing that I can actually beat you in."

Okay, I take back my earlier statement. "Do you care to place a wager on it then?"

"Okay, if I win I get kiss."

"And if I win? What do I get?"

"What would you like?"

"Another date."

"Deal."

"I think we should seal this with a kiss." Callie rolls her eyes but stands up on her tiptoes.

"Just a peck, because I want a real kiss when I beat you on that track," she whispers against my lips before placing a quick kiss. Before I know it, she's taking off toward one of the carts. "Last one at the end is a rotten egg," she yells. The little minx is cheating.

"Hey, wait up." I take off after her. Just as I'm getting in my kart, I see her take off. Awe, hell.

Callyn

Hell yeah I cheated. I mean, I'm sure I could have beaten him fair and square, but I want to kiss him, and he's still getting another date anyways. I push the pedal down as far as it would go, taking the turns sharply. I know I have a few feet lead over Zeke. The course isn't long, and the finish line is just up ahead. I'm going as fast as I can, but I will the kart to go faster. I swear it feels like the kart actually does. I start to giggle; my ponytail whipping in the wind behind me. Out of the corner of my eye, I see a go-kart has almost caught up to me. I look over and see that it's Zeke.

How did he catch up to me? I had too far of a lead. There's no way he caught up to me that fast. *Come on, come on, come on. Go faster.* I look back over to Zeke. He has this smug smile on his face. Next thing I know, he's ahead of me, crossing the finish line first. We both bring our karts to a stop. I cross my arms and pout. I should have won. He shouldn't have beaten me.

"Aww, come on Callie, don't be a sore loser."

"How did you beat me? I was too far ahead. There is no way you should have been able to catch up."

"I've been doing this a long time, and you drive like Graydon." I scoff. "Well, you do." He holds out his hand waiting to help me out of the kart. I sigh and take his proffered hand. Once I step out of the kart, he pulls my body into his, wrapping his arms around me. "I'll let you in on a little secret. Don't start off going pedal to the metal. When you take your turns, it's going to take you longer to correct yourself." File that away for next time. "Now, about that date you owe me. You and me next Saturday afternoon. I figured we stay in and watch a movie."

"Do I get cuddles?"

"All the cuddles you can handle."

Hm. Just Zeke and I snuggled together. Oh, the possibilities. "That sounds wonderful."

"And because you're cute and you agreed to my date, how about if I give you your part of our deal... a kiss." He leans down and captures my lips with his. The kiss is just as sweet as he is.

Zeke

"Hey, can you two lovebirds take that off the track, you're holding everyone up." Callie pulls back enough to look up at me, she giggles and smiles.

"Come on. There is one more thing I want you to try here." I take her hand and lead her to the paint drum. "You're gonna want to take your jacket off for this." She shrugs off her jacket, handing it to me. "Okay, now you're going to take the drumsticks and when the music starts playing beat the sticks in the center of the drum in front of you." She nods. This is going to be fun.

Nirvana's "Smells Like Teen Spirit" starts playing. She couldn't have gotten a better song. I take my phone out of my pocket, pulling up the camera. The first hit on the drum splashes paint in the air, landing in various places on her. I capture the shocked expression on her face. Callie looks at me and gives me this big beautiful smile. It lights up her whole face. She couldn't have looked more gorgeous if she tried.

Callie really starts getting into it, jumping around, hitting the drum to the beat. I start to record her. Later on, I'm going to edit the video and put part of it in slow-mo. It's going to look amazing. The song ends, and Callie places the drumsticks on the drum, walking over to me with the biggest smile on her face.

"You have no idea how much I want to hug you right now." I open my arms. I'm not bothered by the paint one bit. It gives her all she needs, and in the next second, she is in my arms. Right where she is supposed to be.

Chapter 10

Lucian

We've been waiting all weekend to hear what my grandfather had to tell us. I'm usually all for school, but I wanted this day to be over, so we can get our news. When the last bell rang for the day, all of us rushed to the car to get to my house as fast as we could. Now, we're waiting for my grandfather to come home; which should be any minute. We're all waiting in the living room while my grandmother is in the kitchen, cooking dinner.

"Lucian." I turn and look at Zeke. "Do you have any idea what your grandfather is going to tell us?"

"All I know is that he has some good and bad news but didn't want to go into detail until all of us were together. He wanted to do it this weekend, but I explained to him what was going on, and he agreed to wait until tonight. He said that it would give the guys he sent to Riverwalk a chance of getting back to him, and he could possibly have more information about Lorcan's descendant."

"Am I the only one who is tired of calling him that? I mean damn how hard is it to find out his name," Max interjects.

"For once, I agree with Max," Graydon states.

"Well, color me surprised. Callie you might want to write this down. Graydon agrees with me about something." Graydon crosses his arms and glares at Max.

"I can just as quickly change my mind."

"Don't do that. This is a historic moment."

"It's about to be your last."

"Enough," I yell. "Can we all be serious for a second? We have too much going on for us to be acting this way."

"He's right," my grandmother says from the kitchen doorway. "This is a time that all of you need to be on the same page, to band together and be stronger than ever. Quite frankly, I'm tired of all the bickering. Now, you either put your differences aside, or if you can't, you can get the hell out. Callyn doesn't need this kind of distraction, none of you do. You all have enough on your plates and inside fighting, even over stupid shit, isn't doing any of you any favors."

"Your grandmother is right," my grandfather says.

I didn't hear him come in, but when my grandmother starts talking you shut up and listen, and don't you even think about talking above her, you'll just make it worse.

"Since you're all here, we're just going to get right to it. I've been in contact with the neighboring towns and some of the other councils. I made them aware of the situation. Once they talked to their people, they got back to me, and those who are willing to fight are going to be coming, in waves. Some are staying behind to protect those who can't or won't fight."

"What are they doing to the ones who won't fight and are capable?" I question.

"They are being monitored. The last thing we need is for more of them to start following this unnamed person. Which brings me to the next bit of news. The two scouts I sent to Riverwalk, there's good and bad news. Bad news is, they still haven't laid eyes on him, and they have no clue how big his army really is. They've only seen a handful of people, but we would be remiss to think that is all he has."

"He has a base of operation somewhere."

"Yes, Callie."

"Sooo, we have to find out where it is." Max says

"Yes. It would be a great advantage to us if we did. We could take out a lot of his army and gain the upper hand."

"What about the witch? Do we have any information on her?" Callie asks.

"We have a bit more on her. She is the one walking around town asking about you. She's trying to pass herself off as a relative of yours and that she is trying to find you."

"Well, no one should be able to give her much information. I didn't go anywhere besides school and the grocery store. Though why would she need to ask around about me. If we can find them by a simple location spell, couldn't she just do the same?"

"My guess would be that she has, and she knows exactly where you are. I think it's more of her trying to see who you were associated with and if they are on your side. Now, since you didn't know who and what you were until you came here, there shouldn't be a problem. We also have a picture of her. We can distribute that around and have everyone keep an eye for her. Once she sets foot in this town, we'll know. We just have to be ready for her, for them."

"I don't understand. Why not just come here? He should be strong enough, especially with the help of a witch," I state.

"It's all a power play. He won't get his hands dirty unless it's his last resort. They always try to get others to do their dirty work for them. When their carefully laid plans come crashing down, *that's* when he'll strike, *that's* when he'll show his face."

"So, what's the good news then?"

"As of right now, there are no signs of them making any moves against us. Now, that doesn't mean that he doesn't have plans in the works. But this gives us time to train as many of the new people as possible. We may have a fighting chance." My grandfather gets up and walks to the kitchen.

"Graydon, we're going to have to talk to your father about using the gym to train. We may have to find a bigger area. Callie, you're gonna have to talk to Alcina and we're going to have to start training with her."

"I'll message her now." I nod.

We have to prepare. With this guy's power, let alone the witch's, we need to have a power play on our side, because I don't think that we're powerful enough to take them on.

Callyn

Me: Hey.

Alcina: Hi. Is there something you needed?

Me: We feel like we should start training with you.

Alcina: How do you plan on doing that? I'm a witch.

Me: I know, but we have to find a way to work together, to make us all stronger.

Alcina: I understand that, but I don't know how to go about that.

Me: We don't either, but we have to try.

Alcina: Ok. Let me know when and where.

Me: I will. Also, we have a picture of Circe, and we learned a couple of things about Lorcan's descendant.

The air pressure changed and Alcina stood before me.

"Do we have a name?"

"Not yet. Apparently, he is in hiding and having Circe and his followers do his bidding."

"I figured as much. Can I see the picture?"

"Lucian, can you get your grandfather's phone? I want to show Alcina Circe's picture."

It only takes him a moment before he is placing the phone in my hand, the picture already on the screen. I turn the phone toward Alcina. She gasps the second she sees the picture.

"This can't be," she whispers.

"What?"

"She shouldn't be alive. She looks just like the painting I've seen of her. No one is supposed to live that long. Yes, magical beings and shifters tend to live longer than a human, but not to this degree."

"Are you saying what I think your saying?"

"Yes, this is Circe, she was alive over two hundred years ago."

"How is this possible?"

"Very dark magic, blood magic. Let's just say that once you go down that path, there is no coming back from it. The things you have to do..." she shudders. "You were right when you said we need to find a way to make us stronger. I thought Circe was a relative from the one two hundred years ago, but it's not. She will have gained two hundred years of experience and magical knowledge. We need to get started soon, or we may all be doomed."

Great just what we need a two hundred-year-old power tripping witch and a long lost relative on a revenge trip. Both with insurmountable power. How the hell are we going to beat that?

Chapter 11

Callyn

We're not waiting to start training with Alcina. We're starting tonight after school. Cat is going to be there. I called her late last night to let her know what was going on. I'm hoping we can come up with some kind of plan. Alcina said she was going to do some digging and see if she can find some spell or information on how to combine our powers. She thinks it's the only chance we got, and she's probably right. Unless, we find the talisman and break it, or we figure out a way to get Circe out of the picture; the odds are stacked against us. We're not going down without a fight.

"Any word yet from Alcina?" Lucian asks.

"No. I'm not sure if that's a good thing. She seems to think that Circe and my relative's powers are separate, that they're not connected in any way. She also said she's not aware of any spell that can combine our powers with hers. I hope she's wrong and finds something."

"Yes, the sooner we know the better."

"My father and the rest of our parents are going to be the ones training the new people. He said there's no way we could do it and train ourselves," Graydon states as he sits down at our usual lunch table. "Depending on the amount of people that show up, we may not have a choice. I say we get as much training in as possible before we have to help train the new people."

"Does anyone know when the first wave of people are supposed to be coming?"

"Soon. Probably by the end of the week. At least, that's what my grandfather said."

"I have a question, but it's for Callie."

"What's that, Max?"

"Did you have fun this weekend?"?

"I had a blast. We need to do that again, but I want to do something as a group this weekend. I can't do anything Saturday, but we should try to do something Sunday if everyone can."

"What are you doing Saturday?" Graydon asks.

I look at Zeke and he winks at me. "Well, Zeke and I have a date."

"When did this happen?" Graydon crosses his arms waiting for my answer.

"It was part of bet we had when we raced go-karts. If I won, I got a kiss, and if he won, he got another date. He won. You can't be mad at him because he beat you to it."

"I was unaware that you going to be accepting dates so soon after all the information that just came out and all the training we have to do," Graydon growled.

"My life isn't going to stop just because someone is trying to kill me. We had this planned out before Elder Harris told us anything. It was set the night of our first date. Don't you dare throw a tantrum over this."

"A tantrum, that's what you think I'm going to do?" his voice rising.

"Well, if the shoe fits." I glare at him. He stands abruptly, his chair falling behind him.

"If that's what you think, then I'll go. It's clear I'm the only one worried about your safety. But by all means, if you want to put yourself out in the open and make yourself an easier target, go for it. I'm out." Graydon grabs his things and leaves before I can stop him.

"What does he mean by he's out? Is he leaving me? Is he done being my mate? Is he not going to help us?" I ask as I look around the table. Everyone looks as shocked as I feel.

"I don't know, but you need to go find out. Don't worry about your stuff, I'll bring it to class for you," Zeke says.

I nod. I'm up and out of my seat in a flash. I dart out of the cafeteria and look both ways down the hallway, but I don't see him. *Where could he have gone? Think Callie.* I start moving the direction of our next class, since we're in there together. That would be the logical answer. I stop in the middle of the hallway. Wait, we're bonded, I can try to silently communicate with him.

Graydon? Nothing. *Graydon, please answer me.* Still nothing. I feel the tears welling up in my eyes. I start walking toward our class, hoping that he's there. I try to silently communicate with him again. *Graydon.* This time I don't keep the desperation out of my voice. Just when I think he's not going to answer me, he does.

What do you want Callie?

Where are you? I want to talk to you.

Where do you think?

Class?

Yeah. I can feel the sigh in his answer.

Okay, I'm almost there.

I need to make this right. I can't...no I won't lose him. He's not getting rid of me that easy.

Graydon

I don't need to look up to see who entered the room. I would have known it was Callie even if she hasn't told me she was on her way here. I can feel her energy, let alone smell her scent. She can't blame me for getting pissed a little bit ago. We all took a chance over the weekend with her safety. I don't feel comfortable doing it again so soon. I wasn't going to sit there and argue with them because I know they all would have taken her side. So, I stopped the conversation before, what did Callie call it? Oh yeah, before I could throw my tantrum. What am I, five? She knows I'm grumpy, and I'm going to be the one that's going to tell her like it is. I'm not going to sugar coat things for her. Her life...all of our lives are in danger. I'm not going to be the one to keep risking it.

"Graydon, will you look at me?" I really didn't want to. I cross my arms but keep my eyes focused on my desk. I heard her walk up to me. I felt the weight of her gaze, but I purposely didn't look at her. "Please Graydon." I hear the tremble in her voice and my resolve almost breaks, but she needs to learn she can't get her way with everything. "Please, just talk me. I don't want you to leave me. I don't want you to stop being my mate."

My head snaps up. What the hell does she mean stop being her mate? I didn't say that. Why the hell would I stop? I love her stubborn ass too much. I take a moment to look her, at her posture. Her hands are buried in the sleeves of her shirt, her eyes downcast, but I can still see the tears running down her cheeks. I haven't seen this side of Callie in a long time, not since we first meet her. Fuck, I think I just screwed this up.

"Callie bear," I say softly. "What are you talking about? I'm never going to stop being your mate."

"Really?" she hiccups.

"Yes, really. Come here."

She walks around the desk; I turn to the side, so she is in front of me. I reach out, pushing up her sleeves so I can grab her hands. I pull her towards me, letting go of her hands to place them on her waist. Her hands go to my shoulders.

"Why do you think I'm going to stop being your mate?"

"Be-because you said you were out. I thought that meant you were done with all of this, with me."

"Callie, I'll never be done with you. Do you realize how much you mean to me? You give me a purpose, a reason to strive to be better. I didn't mean that I was leaving you when I said that. It just meant that I was done with that conversation. You guys weren't going to listen to me. You know as well as I do that they would have taken your side no matter what. I was getting frustrated, so I left. I never meant for you to take it as I was leaving you. The only way that is happening is if I die and not even then. I'll haunt you and be your grumpy bear ghost. I love you Callyn Silvers, don't you ever forget that."

She nods her head, wraps hers arms around my neck and bear hugs me. Actually, more like she almost chokes me to death, but I'm not about to stop her.

"I love you too, Graydon. I'd be lost without you," she whispered against my neck.

Callie hugs me a second more before she releases me, pulling back to look into my eyes. I hate the fact that I made her cry. I'm such an ass. I move my hands, cupping her face. I use my thumbs to wipe away the tears.

"I hate seeing you cry, and I hate that I'm the reason. Can you forgive me Callie bear?"

"I already did." I pull her face down towards mine and kiss her.

"Aww. The love birds kissed and made up." I pull back sighing. Max.

"How long have you been out there? You all might as well come in because I know the rest of you are out there too."

"We've been here the whole time. Do you think that we would have let her come by herself?" Zeke growls.

"We're her back up." Max grins. "Just in case you decided not to get your head out of your ass. You're crazy if you think we would let her walk in here to take more of that. Plus, if you were stupid enough to leave her, we were going to be here to pick up the pieces, right after we beat the hell out of you."

I nod. "It would have been deserved."

"Just to clarify, the date she agreed to was her coming to my house to watch movies," Zeke states.

Some of the tension left my body, and I knew Callie felt my shoulders relax.

"It was never about the date, was it?" Callie questions.

"No."

"It was the thought of me going out in town that bothered you the most."

I shrug my shoulders. What can I say, she's not wrong.

"Well, in that case, if anyone else wants to ask Callie out, make sure it's a home date." Max leans closer to Callie, his voice dropping. "I can think of plenty of things we can do in my bedroom, angel."

A growl escapes my lips, but what does Callie do? She bites her bottom lip and smiles. Could she be ready to move our relationship to the next level? I hope so, because it's getting harder and harder not to take things further.

"Let's go Max. The end of lunch bell is about to ring, and we don't want to be late for class," Lucian interjects.

"If I must. Later, angel."

"Bye, guys." She turns and looks at me. "I should probably sit in my own seat."

She should, but I don't want to let her go just yet. "Are we okay? I'm sorry for hurting you; I didn't mean it."

"I know you didn't. We're okay."

Reluctantly, I let her go. She must sense my unease because she reaches over and grabs my hand, giving it a squeeze. I would do anything for her. I promised I would keep her safe, and I will. Even if she hates me for it.

Chapter 12

Catori

Training tonight isn't going so great. They've added Alcina to the mix, saying that she shouldn't just rely on her magic in a fight. I agree, but she has a long way to go. I wasn't sure what to think when Callie texted me about them training with Alcina. She searched for some spell to help enhance theirs and her powers more. I guess she found a spell and is waiting to try it out at the end of practice. You can bet your sweet ass I'm staying to keep an eye out on my best friend.

She also told me about the new people that are going to be coming in. I cringe. That didn't go so well for us the last time. I hope that this time will be different. Graydon's voice booms across the gym.

"Come on, Alcina. You can do better than that."

Is it wrong to say I get a sick sort of satisfaction watching him yell at her? I know he's doing it with good intention, but still. I honestly thought she was going to give up after the first five minutes, but she's hanging in there. She's tougher than she looks. I'll give her that much. After a few more minutes, Graydon calls the end of practice.

"Ten-minute break, then we're going to try that spell. I think we should do it outside because we don't know what will happen, and I don't want to have to explain to my father how we burned his gym down if something goes wrong."

Callie walks up to me. "So, what did you think?"

"It could have been worse." I shrug. "She has a long way to go, but it will be better for her in the long run."

"Are you staying for the next part?"

"Damn straight I am."

"Good. You know, just in case." I understand what she means. Just in case Alcina tries any funny business, but I'll take that bitch down if she tries anything.

"Don't worry. I got your back."

"I know you do. Come on, we both know Graydon only means five minutes and not ten. I saw him go outside already with Alcina." Graydon isn't very patient, but he's gotten a little better since he met Callie.

I follow her outside. We walk a little way to the woods that are behind the gym. Alcina is setting up for the spell.

"Everything is ready. I want to try it first without the blood."

"Is there really a difference?" Lucian questions.

"Yes. Blood always makes the spell stronger. I don't like doing that unless it's absolutely necessary. Blood magic is hard to come back from once you start doing it. All that power is enticing to some."

Hm. She earned a few more points in my book for that honesty.

"Stand back, just in case."

All of us take a few steps back. We all watch in fascination as Alcina starts to mix ingredients in a bowl, referring to the book that lays open next to her. She starts to say the spell, adding different things as she goes. After she was done, I was a little disappointed. I kind of expected it to be a bit flashier. You know like a few flames or at the very least some sparks. But nothing happens.

"Um, does that mean the spell didn't work?" I ask.

"One way to find out." Alcina stands and looks at the Callie and the guys. "Which of you want to give this a try?"

Zeke steps forward. "I will. Out of all of us, my elemental power should be the least destructive if something goes wrong."

I watch as Zeke pulls moisture from the air, a small ball of water hovers just above his hand. Alcina hovers her hand above the water ball but nothing happens. She then places her hand on his arm, but again, nothing happens.

"Are you sure you're doing this right? What is this spell even supposed to do?" Alcina glares at me. "Give me dirty looks all you want, it's not going to change anything."

"We can try to do the spell again but add drops of our blood."

"I don't know if we should trust this. Nothing happened before, and I doubt anything will happen now. I don't understand why we're wasting our time with this. As far as I can tell, this does nothing for you. Aren't we supposed to make *you* stronger? We're fine with the five of us. Callie is *our* catalyst. We're stronger together. From what I can see, you're the weak link here, not us," Graydon yells.

"I'm just trying to help, like you asked," she hisses.

"You're not getting our blood. No way are we walking down that path. If you truly want to help, find another way," Graydon growls.

"Fine. I'll try to find another way."

"Thank you," Lucian says.

The others start walking back into the gym, but Callie stops in front of me.

"Thank you for staying."

"Of course. Look, I know I said we could trust her, but have Zeke use his ability later just to make sure. We already know that talismans can siphon power, who's to say she didn't just do that too."

She sighs. "I will."

"Go on. I'll stay out here and keep an eye on her."

"Do you want me to stay with you?"

"No, I got this."

"I'll wait inside for you."

I nod. I focus my attention on Alcina who is in the process of cleaning up. I need to touch her or something of hers to see if I have another vision. I can have visions without any touching, but they're stronger when I do. Sighing, the only way to do that is to go over and help her. Accidently touching her would go over better than being obvious. Alcina looks up at me as I approach her.

"Did you come over here to doubt me some more?"

"I came over to help, but you can't blame me for doubting you. Yes, I said you could be trusted, but what kind of friend would I be if I didn't tell them to be careful. I'm only looking out for Callie's best interest, and a part of that is trying to help her find a way to change that vision."

"What do you think I'm trying to do? I don't want Circe to be in control. You have to be out of your mind if you think she's not pulling some strings, especially that of whoever is helping her."

"What makes you say that?"

"I haven't seen or heard of a witch that started using blood magic who wasn't out for power. For her to still be alive after two hundred years, she is using some serious blood magic. One way to keep whatever is sustaining her flowing, she had to make a deal with someone, and that someone is Lorcan's descendant. She's had to have promised him power, but Circe will turn on him. Those who want power only want more once they get a taste, and they will do anything to it get it, even turn their backs on their allies."

"If that's the case then why would she attack Callie and the guys?"

"My guess would be because she wants them out of the way before she takes out Lorcan's descendant, leaving her with all the power."

"You know an awful lot about this. What do you think she is going to do with all of that power?"

"You hear things when you're around other witches. I've heard this happening with other people. It's only logical to reason she wants to rule over everyone. That was the original plan when the talisman was created all those years ago."

"Well then, we're screwed."

"Looks that way now, but anything can happen."

I reach over, picking up the book she was using, when I started to get the feeling that I usually do right before I have a vision.

"Be careful with that, it's..." Alcina's voice trails off as I'm thrust into a vision.

"We're going to be making a move soon. Is everything ready?"

"Almost, just a few more people to put into place."

"Excellent."

"Yes, they are blissfully unaware that we are so close. They're children trying to play a game that I'm much better at."

"You couldn't do this without me."

"Oh, Amos, when are you going to realize that the only reason you have power is because of that necklace. Without it, You. Are. Nothing." Circe trails a finger down Amos' chest. "Your only job is to keep that necklace safe. Don't forget, I can end you." Circe walks out of the room.

"You bitch," he yells. "I knew I shouldn't have trusted her." He walks over to a desk, unlocking a drawer. He pulls out a box, opening the lid. There, inside, is Celtic knot necklace with a hexagon shaped ruby. "It'll be a cold day in hell before I let her get her hands on this."

I blink my eyes to see Alcina in front of me.

"You okay?"

I nod. "Yeah, but I have to go tell Callie something. You should come to." I race into the gym and seeing Callie and her mates in the center of the room. "I know his name."

"Hell yeah," Max fist bumps.

"That's not all. Circe and Amos aren't getting along, and they're planning to make a move soon."

"Fuck," Graydon says.

"I saw it."

"Saw what?"

"The necklace, the talisman. It's locked in a drawer, in a desk, wherever he is hiding."

"We need to draw him out."

"I think the only way to do that is to defeat whatever is coming our way," Lucian states.

"We need our help here *now* because we don't know how long we have before they strike."

All of us nod our heads in agreement. We need to band together because go time is almost here.

Chapter 13

Zeke

The rest of the week passed by in a blur. Between classes and training, there hasn't been a moment to spare. Once we told Elder Harris, he made sure to speed up the process on getting people here to train. So far so good. There haven't been any incidents, but we're still keeping a close eye on them.

There was little fight between us guys about me and Callie still doing our date today, but I won. Callie should be here any minute. I rub the back of my neck. There is no reason to be nervous. Callie has been here plenty of times. Well, this will be the first time we'll be here alone...in my room. I glance around the room making sure it's clean. I have my laptop ready. All I need is to grab drinks and snacks.

There is a knock on the door. I run down the stairs, taking a deep breath, before I open the door. Callie looks amazing in her jeans and hoodie.

"Come on in." *Don't be lame. Relax.* Callie gives me a smile.

"Are we still watching movies today?"

"Yup. I just have to grab some drinks and make some popcorn."

"Is your mom here?"

"No. She left for work already, so it'll just be us. Are you okay with that?"

"Yeah. Why wouldn't I be?"

"Okay," I say as I exhale.

"I'll help you grab stuff. What movie are we watching?"

"I figured I'd let you pick." I pop a bag of popcorn in the microwave. "We can pretty much pick whatever you want. There are a ton of apps."

"What is your favorite movie?"

"I watch everything, but comedy and action are usually my favorite.

I really like "Sabotage" it's a great action movie. My favorite comedy slash action movie would have to be "Deadpool". The second one came out, but I haven't gotten a chance to see it yet."

"Well, then I would like to watch the movies you like."

"I have to warn you there is a lot of shooting and killing in both movies."

"And?"

I shake my head. "Nothing, I was just warning you."

The microwave goes off; I grab the bag and shake it, hoping to pop one or two more kernels. Callie grabs the big bowl that was left out on the counter, placing it in front of me. I dump the popcorn in the bowl, and she grabs the bottles of water. She starts to head toward the living room.

"Um, Callie...um I thought we could watch the movies upstairs...in my room." Her eyes open wide. "Or we don't have to. We can watch them down here if that would make you feel more comfortable," I stammer.

She clears her throat. "Upstairs is fine. It just caught me off guard."

I head to the stairs, hesitating for a moment. We should probably watch them down here. I don't want to give her the wrong idea.

"It's fine Zeke." Callie walks around me and starts going up the stairs. "Come on. Let's go watch some movies."

Callyn

I knew why Zeke didn't move, but I know that he would never do anything that I didn't want to do. It just surprised me, because when I usually come over, we stay downstairs. I've seen his room, but when I'm in there his mom is home. It's going to be a little weird being in there when she's gone. I knew what Zeke was going to say, so I took the choice from him. After a few seconds, he starts to follow me up the stairs.

"Um, you can put the water on the stand along with the popcorn."

I do that, then I take my hoodie and shoes off. "Do you care what side I take," I say as I gesture to the bed.

"N-nope."

I smirk. "Fine. Then, I'm taking the side by the snacks." He nods. I jump on his bed trying to break the tension. "Man, your bed is really soft." Zeke still hasn't said anything. I look over at him and see him taking in some deep breaths. "Look, we can go back downstairs if this is too much."

"I just need a minute."

"Okay." While Zeke does that, I take the time to rearrange his pillows to prop myself up. Eventually, Zeke finally sits down on the bed. "So, which movie are we watching first?"

"Sabotage."

He pulls up the movie, I scoot closer to him, and grab the bowl of popcorn. It takes him until we're about a third of the way through the movie before he relaxes and sits back against the headboard. I take the opportunity to put the bowl of popcorn on his lap and snuggle against him. Zeke tenses for a second before moving his arm around me. I don't think he realizes, but he starts to play with my hair which turns into him rubbing his hand, where he can reach, up and down my arm.

Don't boyfriend and girlfriends make out while watching movies, because we should definitely do that. My fingers start to play with the buttons on his shirt. I've totally forgotten about the movie. His hand stills. I feel him shift slightly.

"Callie," he whispers. I move back enough that I can look up at him. "What are you doing?"

"Trying to get your attention."

"It's working."

"Good. Aren't we supposed to be making out?"

"We can."

I shift higher to make it easier to reach his lips. He places the bowl of popcorn on his stand, turning, he pulls my body on top of his. One of his hands goes behind my head, pulling me closer. There is no hesitation on his part. His lips meet mine. This kiss feels different, this feels like more. I'm excited to see where this takes us.

Zeke takes my leg and moves it over his waist, causing me to shift so that I am straddling him. He runs his hands down my back, gripping my butt. I move my hands to the hem of his shirt, pushing my hands underneath it. I've been itching to get my hands on his skin.

"Callie, wait," Zeke says against my lips. I sit up looking at his face. His eyes are shut tight, and his hands are clenched. "I need to get up for a second." The second I move, he is up and off the bed.

"Did I do something wrong?"

"No. God, no. I just needed you to stop because I was a few seconds away from throwing you down on my bed.

I make my way off the bed and stand before him. "Maybe, I didn't want you to stop."

"Callie, you don't know what you're asking."

"Yes, I do. I may not be experienced but I know what I want, and I want you."

Zeke

I start pacing. When I invited Callie over to spend time with just me, I didn't think that I would be getting ready to have sex with my mate. I'm nervous. I know this is her first time, she just said as much, but it's mine as well. I'm a guy, I should know what I'm doing, but I don't. What if I mess this up? I mean your first time should be special. Is my bedroom on a whim really special? I can't do this; I shouldn't do this, but God help me, I can't stop.

I turn to look at Callie, I can see the nervousness on her face. "We don't have to do this. We can wait."

"Do you not want to?"

"I do, but I won't rush you if you're not ready." I see her shoulders visibly relax. She takes a deep breath, squares her shoulders, and looks at me.

"No, I want to do this. I'll admit I'm nervous, but I want this, with you."

I close the few feet of space between us. "I'll try to make this special for you."

"It already is," she whispers.

"We'll figure this out together."

I push her hair behind her ear, cupping the side of her face, using my thumb sweeping it over her cheek. I lean down and brush my lips over hers. I move my arms, wrapping them around her waist, pulling her body flush with mine, deepening the kiss. I run my tongue over her bottom lip, lightly nipping, getting the reaction I want. She gasps, parting her lips just enough that I can slip my tongue in her mouth. I glide my hands to her waist, lifting her. She understands what I want when she wraps her legs around my waist.

I place one arm around her waist, my other hand fisting the hair at the nape of her neck. I walk backwards until my legs hit the bed. Gently as I can, without breaking my hold on Callie, we fall back on my bed. I break the kiss, moving back just enough that I can look into her eyes. I can see the desire in them, but there is also some nervousness. I'm sure she can the see the same in my eyes.

Her hands on my waist move up, raising my shirt in the process. I shiver at the feel of her hands on my body. Callie's hands don't stop. She keeps pushing my shirt higher. Removing my hands from where they are, I straighten until I was straddling her. Reaching up, behind me, I gather my shirt in my hands and pull it over my head. Callyn's eyes roam over my shirtless torso. She lifts her hands and starts to reach out to me, but then pulls them back down toward her body. Before she could get too far, I grab her hands and place them on my chest.

"Never be afraid to touch me."

That was all she needed to hear because her hands start to roam my body, touching any and everywhere she can reach. God, I love the feel of her hands on my body, on my skin. All I want to do is put my hands on her body. To feel the touch of her skin under my fingertips. She scoots back enough so she can sit upright. She twists her fingers in the hem of her shirt before crossing her arms and lifting the shirt over her head.

There she sits in a plain, pink, cotton bra, blue jeans and her hair slightly messy, looking as beautiful as ever. I can't wait one more second. I move forward, crawling on my hands and knees, up her body, the few inches that separate us. She scoots back down. I make sure to keep my weight off of her; the majority of my body resting on my left side. My hand starts to shake as I reach for her. Sure, I've touched her before, but not like this. I'm nervous.

Tentatively, I caress Callie. Her skin feels like silk. I run my fingers up and down her body. Stopping at the waistband of her jeans before traveling them back up. I lean down, capturing her lips. Callie wraps her arms around my neck pulling me more firmly on top of her. Nothing has felt better than the feel of her skin on mine. I roll us over, so she is laying on top on me. I run my hands up and down her back, as I continue to kiss her.

My hands pause on the back strap of her bra, feeling the clasp beneath my fingers. How the hell does thing come off? Trying to be inconspicuous as possible, I start to fumble with her strap, and for the life of me, I can't get it to open. Who knew this would be so hard? And apparently, I wasn't as stealthy as I thought because Callie pulls back sitting up. She reaches behind her and in a matter of seconds she has the back undone. I reach up and push her straps off of her shoulders, the bra slipping down her arms.

Holy. Shit.

Callyn

I'm so nervous, that I don't know how I'm not shaking. Zeke tentatively lifts his hands, stopping just before he touches my breast. If I didn't know any better, I would say he's just as nervous and unsure, as I am. That thought makes me feel so much better. I finish removing my bra, dropping it off the side of the bed. I meet Zeke's eyes, giving him a nod, letting him know that I want this. He reaches up and cups by breast, gently squeezing.

I bite my bottom lip. I don't hold back the moan when he runs his thumbs over my nipples. His hands move to my hips, holding me so he can sit up, wrapping his arms around me. I love the skin to skin contact. He runs his hands up and down my back, before circling to the front. His finger tips skimming my skin along the top of the waistband. Zeke's fingers stop on the button. He looks up into my eyes asking permission, and I give it to him. He pops the button and pulls down the zipper, wrapping his arms around my waist, twisting us so that I'm lying on my back.

He scoots down my body, leaving kisses in his wake. I feel his hands grip my jeans at my waist. Lifting my hips, I give him the space that he needs to pull them down, taking my underwear with them. In no time, I'm laying before Zeke completely naked. *Why is he just standing there staring? Does he not like what he sees? Okay Callie don't do this, not now.*

"God, you're beautiful," he says in a breathy whisper and I smile.

I watch as he moves his hands, unbuttoning his jeans, shoving them down his hips, his boxers going with them. My heart races at the sight. He's bigger than I thought. Zeke bends down; I can't see what he's doing, but the next thing I know, I hear a thump. I get up and peer over the side of the bed. I start to giggle at the sight I see. Zeke is laying on his back, hands covering his eyes, his pants twisted around his ankles.

"You okay down there?" I ask with a smile. He groans causing me to chuckle. "What happened?"

"I fell trying to get my pants off," he mumbles from behind his hands. "This isn't going how I thought it would."

"Hey," I say as I climb off the bed and kneel in all my naked glory next to him. "I'm glad this isn't perfect. I'm actually relieved. It's taking the pressure off." I move his hands from his face.

I lean down and kiss him, putting all my emotions into it. He groans wrapping an arm around my back, using his other hand to fist the hair at the nape of my neck, pulling my body down on top of his. I move so that I'm straddling him, my core pressing right up against his. Zeke moves his hands, squeezing by butt, pushing me firmer against him causing me to moan. I rock against him. He pulls back from the kiss slightly. Our breaths mingle, coming out in pants.

"Reach in the nightstand drawer there is a box of condoms in there." I sit up, sliding over his cock in the process causing me to moan, but I in reach in the drawer and pull out the whole box. He takes the box from me, opening it, and pulling out one. "How about we try this again but on the bed."

As gracefully as I can, I climb off Zeke and onto the bed. I hear a low growl from behind me. Glancing over my shoulder, I see Zeke staring at my bent over form. I smile, shake my head, and continue until I'm lying on my back in the middle of the bed, just like we started.

Zeke

I hurry and pull my jeans the rest of the way off. I can't believe that I fell trying to get them off in the first place. I mean who trips over their own pants. Hopefully, nothing else goes wrong. I look over and see Callie crawling on the bed, and I can't stop the growl that escapes my lips. Yes, I'm human, but there is still an animal in me, and he loves the sight of her bent over in such a submissive position. I'll have her like that one day, but not today, that will not be how we both share our first times.

I wait for Callie to settle on the bed before I toss the box of condoms on the nightstand. I rip the foil off the one in my hand, trying to roll it over my cock and in the process, I rip the condom. I groan. This shouldn't be this hard. I'm a guy, I should know how to do this. *Get a grip Zeke. Take a deep breath and try again.* I grab the box and take out another foil pack.

Out of the corner of my eye, I see Callie move until she is resting back on her forearms, one eyebrow raised, questioning. I open the foil pack and try again. Don't ask how it happens, but one minute I'm trying to put the condom on, then the next thing I know it gets flicked, and I watch in horror as it hits Callie right in the forehead. She's just staring at me wide-eyed, complete shock on her face. I hang my head in shame.

"And the hits just keep on coming," I sigh.

I don't know what I expected Callie to do, but out right laughing isn't one of them. For a brief moment, I start to think that Callie is laughing at me, but I take a look at her and realize she is laughing at the absurdity of this whole situation. I can't help but join her. I move and flop on the bed next her. We both turn our heads and look at each other.

"Do you think this is a sign that we shouldn't do this?"

"No, I don't think that."

"I wanted this to be perfect for you," I say.

"It is. Yeah, there may be some bumps, but this not going according to plan it the best thing. The whole pressure for this to be perfect is gone."

"Are you sure?"

"Absolutely. How about we try again?"

I smile, reach over and grab another foil pack from the box. I take a deep breath and roll on the condom, this time without any problems. I shift and settle my body between her legs. I make sure that some of my weight is on the forearm resting by her head. I use my thumb, running it across her cheek. Using my other hand, I grip behind her thigh, lifting her leg up higher. I look into Callie's eyes. She gives me a shy smile and slight nod of her head. I position myself so that my cock's at her entrance, praying that I don't screw this up. If one thing is going to go right about this whole situation, please let it be this moment.

I feel Callie's hands on my back, right above my ass. She uses the leg that I'm not holding and presses it closer to my body. I push forward slowly. Callie squeezes my back. In one swift motion, I push all the way inside, her nails digging in my back. She inhales sharply then slowly releases her breathe. My whole body shudders. I have never felt something as good as Callie wrapped around me. It takes everything that I have not to move. I give her a few moments, waiting for a sign that she is ready for me to continue. After what seems like forever, even though it was only a few seconds, Callie nudges me.

"Are you okay?"

"Perfect," she whispers. I pull back and push forward in slow shallow thrust. Her breathy moan sounds next to my ear. "More." I pick up the pace, moving faster and harder. I feel her leaving scratches across my back.

I growl at her small show of dominance. It spurs me on more. I release Callie's leg, and she waste no time wrapping her them around my waist. I plant my hands on either side of her head, pulling my upper body off of her. Callie has her eyes closed, mouth parted open. She looks amazing. The flush of her skin, the sound of her moans, the way her body clutches at mine. I need to see her eyes. I need her look at me as we both get ready to tumble over the cliff.

"Look at me Callie." She opens those beautiful brown eyes.

"Zeke, I'm so close. Please, don't stop." Like I could.

I push into her even faster and harder. I'm glad she's close because

I don't know how much longer I can last. I feel her squeeze around my cock right before she screams. I follow her right over the edge.

Callyn

I see Zeke's arms almost give out. The only sound that can be heard is our breathing, which is coming in slow, short pants. I don't know what I was expecting my first time to be like, but this wasn't it. Yes, there were some mishaps, but it was still perfect. I'm glad we got to experience this together.

"Callie," he whispers.

"I know Zeke, you don't have to say anything."

He leans down giving me one of the most intimate kisses. Next thing I know, he is flipping our positions, lying on his back, with me sprawled over him, rubbing his hand up and down my back. I lay my head on his chest, right over his heart; my hand resting next to my face. I listen to the rhythm of his heart beat for a moment. I move head so that I am looking up at him, resting my chin on my hand. He shifts, so he is looking at me.

I smile. "Let's me know when you're ready for round two."

Zeke chuckles but kisses me senseless. Round two was just as good as the first.

Chapter 14

Callyn

I can't stop thinking about the other night. It's distracting me from everything that I'm supposed to be doing. Right now, I'm supposed to be training and all I can think about is Zeke and how much I want to do that again with him and with the others. I wonder how it will be with the others.

"Callie, focus," Cat says as she snaps her fingers in front of my face. "What has you daydreaming?"

I grab her arm, dragging her to a secluded corner. There are too many shifters in here and I don't want them to overhear.

"You have to promise you won't say thing."

"Like you have to ask."

"Okay, so you know the other day I told you that I had another date with Zeke." She nods her head. "Well, we stayed in. You know, watched some movies, ate some snacks, cuddled a little. Well, one thing lead to another, and we had sex," I whispered.

"Holy shit," she practically yells.

"Ssshhh."

"Shit, sorry. But you have to tell me everything."

"I will, later. I promise."

"Well, at least tell me how it was."

"It was great. It wasn't perfect and there were some mishaps, but he was sweet and caring. I couldn't have asked for more."

Cat pulls me by the shoulders, hugging me. "I'm so glad and happy for you. I want to know all about those mishaps."

"Let's just say, they were funny but lightened the tension." We both start to giggle.

A pair of arms wrap around my waist, pulling me back into a body; a pair of lips land on my cheek. Max. I love his sunshine smell.

"What are you two ladies doing over here in the corner?"

"Oh, just girl stuff, like gossiping."

"Well, when you're done, I need to ask this pretty lady a question."

"How about I just give you two a moment alone. Come find me when you're done Callie, so we can finish our training session." Cat winks at me before she walks away.

I turn in Max's arms, wrapping mine around him. "What did you want to ask me?"

"Would you like to come over my house on Saturday? We haven't pranked Graydon in a while and I figured we could do that and just hang out."

"Sounds like a plan."

"Good." He gives me a peck on the lips. "Now," he spins me around, "I'll let you get your fine ass back to training." He smacks my ass before giving me a slight nudge in the direction that Cat went.

I look over my shoulder. "You know, you're lucky you're so cute."

He pushes his hair behind his ears and winks at me. "Just cute? You wound me."

"I don't need to inflate your ego anymore."

"Love you too, angel."

I shake my head. I'm walking over to Cat when one of the new people comes rushing into the gym.

"The center of town is being attacked. We need to go, now."

The guys and Cat all rush over to me. The rest of the gym starts to file out the front door.

"Did anyone get a message from their parents about this? We need to warn the people out back."

"I'll go tell everyone outside," Alcina says before taking off toward the back door.

"None of us has received any messages," Zeke says.

"I'll call my grandmother."

"Should we go?" I ask.

"She's not answering."

Alcina comes racing back in. "They're on their way."

"Let's go. We're wasting time. Callie, Alcina, and Zeke with me.

Cat you go with Lucian and Max." Graydon's voice leaves no room for arguments.

We all run out to the cars, piling in, taking off the second all the doors were closed.

Graydon?

Yeah?

What the hell are we going to do when we get there? We don't know where or if any of our parents are safe?

I don't know. We're just going to have to wait to see what we're walking into.

That doesn't make me feel any better.

It's not supposed to. Be on guard, check your surroundings, and don't leave our side.

I won't.

Good.

The rest of the ride no one says a word. When we finally get there, which felt more like hours than minutes, we pull up to complete and utter mayhem. Broken glass from nearby buildings litters the street. There are cars on fire, people and animals fighting in the middle of the road. All of us hop out of the car as soon as it's parked. Max and Lucian come running towards us.

"Jesus, this looks like an episode of *When Animals Attack*, Max says. "What the hell are we supposed to do?"

"Let's circle the outside and see if we can spot one of our parents."

Halfway around the riot, we finally spot Graydon's dad.

"Dad!" Graydon yells. "Dad!"

He can't hear us over all this noise. I glance around to see if I have a clear enough path to get to Mr. James. Everyone is occupied with whoever is in front of them that I doubt they realize me and the boys are even here. I take a deep breath and take off running before on the guys stop me.

"Callie!" I hear all of them shout behind me, but I don't stop. I can't.

Graydon

"Callie!" For once, I would love if that girl would actually listen to me. "Guys, we need to go and protect our mate because she decided that running out in the middle of this fight was a good idea." All of us take off after her. She makes it to my father seconds before we do.

"What should we do?" she asks.

"Nothing. I want you boys to take her and leave here. We got this. There are only handful of them left."

"We can't leave you here."

"Yes, you can... and you must. They don't need to see you, any of you." He lightly grips her upper arms. "They came here for you, and we can't let them get their hands on you. Do you understand me? Now, go. We'll talk later. Graydon, take them to our house. You boys listen to me. "Nothing, and I mean nothing, gets through that door to her." We all nod. My dad nods back. "Go!" He walks Callie back until she's in my arms. The second he releases her he takes off in one direction, and I start tugging Callie in the other.

"You can't seriously be leaving them here to defend themselves."

"Yes, we are. You heard what my father said. They are here for you, and I'll be damned if I let them touch you." She starts trying to pull her hand free, but no way am I going to let her go. "My father told me to get you out of here, and goddamn it, that's what I'm going to do. You might as well stop trying to escape."

"Stop just for a minute and hear me out...please."

I stop and take a deep breath. Why did she have to use her soft voice? It gets me every time. I hang my head because I know I'm going to let her say what she wants, but that doesn't mean we're going to do what she wants. I turn to face her, making sure I keep my grip on her hand.

"Fine, you have one minute to say what you want to say, and then I'm taking you home."

"What kind of queen would I be if I didn't stay and fight? These people are here because of me, because they believe in me. This is happening because of me; I can't let them do this on their own. I need to set an example. I *need* to be the queen you and they deserve."

Max groans, and I agree with that sentiment. She's right, but I can't risk it. Not when we have a bigger war to prepare for.

"I hear you, and while I can't argue with what you said, we're still not staying." I turn back around and start tugging back to my truck.

"They need to see me out there. How can we ask people to risk their lives for us, when we're not willing to do the same?"

I growl. "We're leaving, and that's final." A loud squawk has me stopping in my tracks.

"Damn, you really pissed her off. I'd let go before she tries to peck your hand," Max whispers.

I don't get to answer because someone walks up to us.

"So, you're the bitch that has my boss going crazy. I don't see why. You don't look like much. Maybe I should just snap your neck now and be done with all of this." A round of growls can be heard.

I push Callie behind me. "Take one step toward her and you won't live long enough to take another breath."

"Ha-ha-ha. Do you really think that you can take me? You're weak."

This time it's my turn to laugh. "You clearly don't know who or what I am. Please, do me the favor. I haven't had a good fight in a long time. I doubt that you would last more the five minutes against me."

"Why you little... we'll see about that."

The guy shifts, dropping down on all fours as a leopard. I smirk. I shift, letting out a loud roar as I land on my paws. My nose twitches.

"Oh man, he's pissing himself," Max laughs.

I don't have time for this. I move forward and the coward turns, running away. He's not getting away that easy. I lumber after him. He's not making it out of this alive.

Maximus

I can't help the laugh that comes from me as I watch Graydon's big bear ass try to run after a leopard. I don't know what kind of show this Amos guy it is running, but it's not informing his followers who they're going up against.

"Max, stop laughing. Is anyone going to help him? We can't just stand here."

"We can, and we will," Lucian growls. Callie crosses her arms, narrows her eyes as she stares down Lucian down.

"Oh, really?"

Angel, this is not a fight you want right now.

Yes, it is. I'm not going to stand here and do nothing. Screw this and you guys.

Callie, what are you thinking about doing? Callie! Answer me, please.

She doesn't, and the next thing I know, a giant phoenix stands before us. I take a step toward her, but she screeches and launches herself in the air.

"Fuck, Graydon's going to be pissed. We have to follow her. No way I want to be chewed out more than what we are going to get for letting her shift. I'm not getting yelled at for losing sight of her and not helping her too."

"I'll try and help as much as I can. I know a couple of spells to keep them at bay or stunned long enough for you guys to be able to do something about," Alcina states.

"Go for it."

"We need to keep one of them alive. We need to question them and see what else Amos and Circe have in store for us," Lucian says.

"We're wasting time," Cat says before she shifts and takes off in the direction that Callie went.

The rest of us shift and follow after her. We find Graydon and what's left of the leopard. Well, shit he didn't waste any time with that. He shifts back.

"Where the hell is Callie?"

At least she has good timing, because she swoops down and lands in front of us. Sometimes, I forget just how big and magnificent she is as a phoenix. She lets out a mighty squawk, drawing the attention of everyone here. Two shifters run toward her. The wolf reaches her before the fox does. Callie grabs half of the wolf in her beak, using to her talons to hold the other half of it down. She pulls up, literally ripping the wolf in half. The fox tries to move out of her way, but lands in front of me instead. I growl, then lick my chops. The fox lowers to his belly, before rolling over, and turning his neck to the side.

I move closer and clamp my muzzle over his neck. We'll keep this one alive. Out of the corner of my eye, I see Callie shift back. I move my mouth, and shift back, quickly grabbing the fox again by the neck.

"Enough," she yells. "I want to talk to one of his followers."

"We ain't got nothing to say to you."

"Why are you doing this? You have to know he sent you here to die. Did he tell you who we are?" He doesn't answer.

"I take that as a no," I say. "Maybe you should tell him."

"I am the Alpha Queen and these four guards are my mates." His eyes widen. "You have to know that whatever he has you doing, you have nothing to gain from it. Look around you. He sent you all here to be slaughtered. He knew there was no way you could beat us. Now, are you going to talk to us, or are we sending you back to him in pieces?"

"I ain't got nothing to say."

"So, be it. Graydon," she holds out a hand to him, he takes it.

She had to have talked to him silently because the next I know there is a fireball hovering above is hand. Callie places her hand on his wrist and the ball grows in size and in heat. I can feel it from here. What does she plan to do with that?

"Are you sure you have nothing to say?"

"Like I said, I *ain't* saying nothing."

"Graydon, if you don't mind."

She moves her hand and Graydon hurls the giant fireball at the guy. He instantly catches fire. He's doing the stop, drop, and roll method, but it's not doing him any good. His screams are hurting my ears, but luckily, they don't last long. Well, not lucky for him.

"Did she just...did they just...holy hell." I'm stunned. I never would have expected sweet, shy, Callie to command an act like this.

"Are there any other survivors?" she questions.

"I have one," I say. She looks at me and nods.

"Any others?"

"The few that were left, started slipping out after you went after that wolf," Graydon's father says.

"Cowards. Is there anywhere we can put this one and question him?"

"There is a secret room in the basement of the Elder Council building. It's made to withstand any shifter."

"Can you take him there?"

"Of course."

"What about the rest of our parents? Are they safe?" Zeke asks.

"They're fine. They are scattered around here somewhere."

"I'm going to find Elder Harris and send him your way."

"You did good out here tonight kid." Mr. James pulls Callie in for hug and kisses the top of her head. "I wished you would have listened, but you looked like a real queen there. Keep that up, you're going to need it." Mr. James walks over to me and picks up the fox by the scruff of his neck and walks away.

"Are we in the twilight zone, because I'm seeing things tonight I never thought were possible," I say.

Callie's shoulders deflate. "That was one of the hardest things I've had to do."

"This may have been the first, but it won't be the last. That's the price to pay for being a queen. You're gonna have to make hard choices like this," Lucian states.

"If it makes you feel better, you looked hot...a little scary, but still hot."

She shakes her head but smiles. "Only you would think that."

I shrug my shoulders. "I'm not wrong, and the rest of them think it too. They're just too scared to admit it."

"You're probably right, but we really need to find Elder Harris."

"No need to, he's coming this way," Cat says.

"Well, that was easy."

"That was quite the show young lady."

Callie shrugs her shoulders. "I did what I had to."

"Spoken like a true queen."

She smiles. "Graydon's dad is taking one of Amos' followers to the holding cell. Can you question him to see what he knows?"

"I can."

"Thank you." He gives Callie a hug.

"I'm proud of you."

"Thanks," she says, ducking her head.

Elder Harris gives her a quick kiss on the top of her head. "I'll let you know if I find out anything."

"Thanks again, Elder," I say as he walks away.

"What do we do now?" Callie asks.

"We go home and wait."

"Who's going to clean all this up?"

I put my arm around Callie's shoulders, pulling her into my side. "Don't worry your gorgeous head about that. A clean-up crew will come through. Come on, let's get you home."

Chapter 15

Callyn

We didn't get any information from Amos' follower. It was a waste of a couple of days. It seems they aren't privy to anything until a few days before. I didn't really expect him to know anything. If I were Amos, well more like Circe because she seems to be running the show, I would keep everyone blissfully unaware for reasons just like this.

"Callie are you listening to me?" Max asks.

"Sorry, my mind is elsewhere."

"And where would that be?" Max plops down on the couch next to me.

"Where else, on Amos and Circe. I just wish we knew what they were up to. I don't know if Elder Harris has heard anything from his informants because he was so focused on trying to get information out of that shifter. I hate not knowing."

"We all do, but there is no need to stress about it. Whatever they have planned is out of our control right now. The only thing we can do is focus on the here and now, and right now, I want to focus on planning this prank on Graydon. This could just be what we need, a laugh."

"You're probably right."

"I am right, and you know it. Just admit it." Max reaches over and starts tickling my side. I know he's doing it on purpose because of how ticklish I am. I try to scoot away but he just follows me.

"Okay, okay," I say between giggles.

"Say it. I want to hear you say the words." I fall back against the cushions in my struggle to get away from his hands. Max doesn't stop. Instead, he pursues me. I end up on my back with Max hovering above me. He gives me a wink before leaning down. "I wanna hear you say it," he whispers next to my ear. His teeth nip my earlobe.

"You were...you were right," I say breathlessly.

"Good," he says as he pulls back and sits back up. "Now, about that prank..."

Wait, that's it? I sit up. I want him to continue, to keep kissing me, to run his hands over my body.

"Are you not listening *again*? You aren't still thinking about Amos, are you?" I shake my head. "Then what are thinking about?"

"You...and me."

"Why Callie, are you having not so angelic thoughts?"

"Maybe."

"Were you expecting more, because I can make that happen."

I look him in the eyes. He gets up, stands before me, and holds out his hand. I place mine in his, and he leads me upstairs to his bedroom.

"Are you sure this is okay? I don't want your mom yelling at us?"

Max smirks. "They won't be home for awhile. My mom is at a some spa place a couple towns over. My mom forced my dad to go with her so that they can spend quality time together. She says they don't do enough stuff together."

"Maybe they just needed a little break from everything going on here."

He shrugs his shoulders. "Maybe, but enough talking about my parents."

Max picks me up and tosses me on his bed. I giggle, waiting for him to pounce. Instead of following me, he is grabbing pillows from around his room and tossing them on the floor surrounding his bed. I lean back on my elbows, one eyebrow raised, waiting for him to look at me. A couple of minutes later, he is standing at the foot of the bed with his hands on his hips, assessing what I assume is the arrangement of the pillows. Finally, after what seems like forever, Max looks at me.

"What?" he asks, clearly seeing the confusion on my face.

"Um, do you care to explain why you threw all your pillows on the floor?"

"Oh, yeah, see there tends to be accidents and this is not only for my safety, but yours as well."

I sit all the way up, sitting cross-legged in the middle of his bed. "What do you mean by accidents?"

He takes his hands and runs them through his hair, before shoving them in the front pockets of his blue jeans. "Somehow or another I... she... we... kind of always end up falling off the bed. After doing that so many times, you tend to learn to take precautions, hence the pillows."

I frown, opening and closing my mouth like a fish. "Oookay. Um, wouldn't it just be easier to stay on the bed?"

"Now, where's the fun in that?" he says, right before jumps on the bed causing us both to bounce a couple of times. I lose my balance and end up falling backward. Max lands right next to me. I can't help but laugh. Being with Max is always fun, so why should this be any different.

We end up with me on my back and Max on my right side. He places his right leg over mine, propping himself up on his elbow, head resting in his hand, leaning over me. His hair falls forward. I smile up at him and push his hair back behind his ear. I use that as my reason to caress the side of his face. He takes the opportunity to do the same with me.

"Do you know how beautiful you really are?"

I shake my head. "How about you show me."

"With pleasure, angel."

Max closes the few inches that separate us, his lips meeting mine. I wrap my arms around his neck, pulling him closer. He takes his hand, running it down my side until he gets to the hem of my shirt. As he makes his way back up, my shirt lifts. His hand touching the bare skin of my stomach, up my ribcage, running his fingers across the edge of my bra, before cupping my breast giving it a gentle squeeze.

I moan. Max pulls back, breaking our kiss. He continues to pull away from me until he is at the edge of the bed. He can't stop this. I don't want him too. Where is he going? Just when I get ready to ask him, he stands up but turns and holds his hand out to me. Sitting up, I place my hand in his, wondering where he is going with this. It doesn't take me long to figure that out.

Max moves back so I can stand in front of him. Once both of my feet are on the floor, his hands find the hem of my shirt and lifts it over my head. He places a kiss on my lips, but quickly moves to my neck, placing kisses as he continues his path down my body. I watch him as he moves from my collarbone, to the top of my breast, to right above my navel. He is on his knees before me, his hands on the button of my blue jeans.

Max looks up at me. I love seeing the desire in his eyes, the desire for me. But I know what he is silently asking me. I nod my head, giving him the okay. He wastes no time unbuttoning and unzipping my jeans. He tugs them down my hips and legs, helping me step out of them. Now, I stand before Max in my mismatched, cotton bra and underwear. Why didn't I wear something that matched or even sexy? Probably because I don't own any such thing. Max doesn't seem to mind. He can't take his eyes off of me.

"So, fucking beautiful. I can't believe that you're mine."

I bite my lip. All of my guys know how to make me feel beautiful and special. His hands are everywhere. Touching every single bare skin spot available. I watch as he hooks his thumbs in the waistband of my panties, pulling them down. I hear him inhale deeply followed by a soft growl.

"You smell so good. I can't wait to taste you."

Maximus

My hands travel up her body, to her back. I make quick work of unhooking her bra and sliding it down her arms. Picking her up, I toss her back on my bed. This time I follow. I kiss my way down her body, stopping briefly at her nipples before I continue my path, finally getting to the spot that I want.

I wrap my arms around her thighs, keeping her legs pinned open. The first swipe of my tongue has her inhaling sharply. The next couple have her moaning. It wasn't until I started sucking and licking on her clit that I have her arching her back off the bed.

"Max!" she screams as she tries to clamp her legs around my head, her fingers tugging on my hair. I keep going until she starts to relax, loosening her grip on my hair, her legs falling to the side. "That... that was amazing."

"I'm not done yet."

I crawl up her body, leaving kisses in my wake. I hesitate for a moment when I get to her lips because I'm not sure if she would be willing to taste herself on my lips. I search her eyes and lean down, waiting to see her reaction. I don't get one. I capture her lips with mine, kissing the shit out of her. She wraps her legs around my waist, tugging me closer. I pull back.

"Just one second, angel." I reach over to my night stand, open the drawer, and pull out a condom. I sit up, hastily put it on, then settle myself back between her legs. I need to go slow. I don't want to hurt her. The first time always hurt, right? *Deep breath, Max. You can do this. Slow and steady*.

"Are you sure, angel?"

"Yes." Hesitating for just a second; I kiss her as I thrust inside her; hoping to distract her from the pain. I stop my whole-body shakes.

"Damn."

Her legs lock around my waist. I put my face in the crook of her neck; her arms encircle my shoulders. Her fingernails start digging into my shoulders, spurring me to go faster. This isn't how I want us to end. I put my arms underneath her and flip us. Callie stops, pushing up so she is staring down at me. I grip her hips and bounce her up and down, helping her find a rhythm. Her beautiful breasts bouncing above me is a wonderful sight. I flip us once more. Her breathy moans fill the room.

"Faster." I start to pound into her. "Yes."

I'm so close but I need her to come before me. I move my hand bringing it down between us. I don't get the chance to touch her because she uses my momentum against me and flips us. It's not my soft bed that greets my back, it's air. In a split second, I gather Callie close making sure I take the brunt of the fall, which honestly isn't that bad. I mean I did put pillows down and the fall from my bed to the floor is a particularly long one.

"Shit, you okay?" I expected Callie to be shocked but instead she starts laughing. I can't resist I join her.

"Thank God for the pillows."

I smile up at her and shrug my shoulders. She leans down and kisses me. I run my hands up and down her back, before settling my hands on her ass, gently giving it a squeeze. I start to rock her back and forth, picking up where we left off. One of her hand's lands on my pec, the other going to the night stand above me. Lucky for me, I missed hitting my head on that by mere inches. Callie starts to move faster.

"You look so good bouncing on my dick, angel."

Gripping her hips, placing my feet on the floor, I start to thrust up as she rides me. Her moaning is almost my undoing. I go faster. She shatters, her whole body shaking, as she screams out her release. I follow right after. Callie hangs her head. Both of our breathing coming out in pants. She moves her hand from the night stand and knocks the bowl of half eaten popcorn I left there earlier down, right on my head.

"Ouch," I hiss. "Who knew snacks could be so dangerous." I look up and see shock on Callie's face. Her eyes are wide and her hand covers her mouth. It doesn't last long. Her laughter fills the room a second later. It's contagious, and I laugh right along with her.

"At least this time, it wasn't me who got hit in the head."

I sit so fast that Callie almost falls from my lap. "What do you mean this time?"

"Well," she twists her hands in front of her, "Zeke and I had sex and I got hit in the forehead with a condom." I growl.

ZEKE!

Max? Is that you?

Yes, it's me. Who else would it be? You better not have hurt Callie and forced her into having sex with you.

How do you know that we sex, and you know I would never force her into doing something she didn't want to do? How the hell are you talking to me right now? We've never been able to do this.

Shit, I'm so focused on my anger that I didn't realize we were communicating silently. Holy shit.

Just so you know, she told me she was ready; I would never force myself on her. You know me better than that.

I know man, I'm sorry.

Still doesn't explain how you know or how we can do this.

It came up because a bowl of popcorn hit me in the head, and she said at least it wasn't her this time. I asked about it and she told me. I might as well tell you we just had sex.

Do you think that could be the reason for this?

Possibly. I think Lucian might be able to answer that, but that means we would have to tell him. Which then means Graydon will find out, and I don't know how he will take it.

Do we keep this a secret for now?

Yeah. Man, this is so cool though.

Now we'll be able to talk to each other while we fight, and no one will know what we're planning.

Hell yeah. I better go Callie is giving me weird looks.

Later.

"Care to explain what was just going on? You got this far away look on your face."

"Well, I just found out that I can now communicate silently with Zeke."

"But how? You guys have never been able to do that? Try and see if you can reach Graydon and Lucian."

Graydon? Lucian?

I wait a minute, but nothing. "Nope, just Zeke it looks like."

"I wonder why?"

"Well, mine and Zeke's theory is, it's because you had sex with both of us. But Lucian or maybe even Elder Harris would be able to answer that. It could just be because our powers are getting stronger."

"Both are valid points."

"Yup, but for now, I need your sexy ass to help me clean up the popcorn you spilled. Actually, I feel sticky and need a shower. Want to join me?"

She smiles. "You know, suddenly, I'm feeling dirty. I think I will join you."

Let's just say the shower lasted longer than intended.

Lucian

We're sitting at the diner in town, talking about what our next move is going to be, when Kelsey walks in with some guy I've never seen before on her arm.

"Guys look at the door," I say.

"Damn."

"Is it just me or is anyone else getting the sense of dèjá vu?" Max whispers.

"I'm surprised she would even show her face in this town again. She's not welcome."

"Until we officially take over, we don't have a say, Graydon." He grunts. "It's not that I don't agree with you because I do."

"You're being awfully quiet over there, angel." We look at her awaiting her answer.

It takes a second, but I see her face slowly morph. Shock was there at first, but her eyes narrow, rage and anger taking over. I feel her body tense next to mine, and if she wasn't sandwiched between me and Graydon, I have no doubt that she would be out of her seat and in Kelsey's face. I know the last time she ran into her, Kelsey tucked her tail and ran. I wonder if she is going to do to the same now? I realize that the diner is quiet, everyone is staring at the door.

"Let me out Graydon," Callie growls.

He grunts again. "Not happening."

"Graydon James, you let me out now!" she yells. Everyone in the diner turns and looks at her and then back at Kelsey, who is now making her way over to our table. She stops directly in front of us.

"What the hell do you want? You should have known better than to show your face around here again. And who the fuck is that?" Graydon bellows.

The guy with her pushes her behind him. He wouldn't stand a chance against us. Kelsey steps around him, placing a hand on his arm.

"I didn't come here to start anything. I promise."

"Then why are you here?" Callie snaps.

"I came here to apologize."

"Why? You have to know we would never accept it," Graydon states. "And you have yet to answer my last question, who is this?"

"This is Liam, my mate."

I inhale trying to place what kind of shifter he is, but I can't get a read on him.

Callie, can you smell what kind of shifter he is? She inhales. She turns, wide eyes on me.

He isn't.

Let the others know.

"Well, well, well. It looks like the tides have turned," Max says.

"Does he know?" I question.

"About shifters? Yes. He knows what I am, what most of the town is. He came in with the last wave of people that are here to train."

"Why would they send a human?"

"Because, I was raised by shifters. The family that adopted me believes in her, in you all. I'm here to fight with them. They're my family."

Callie and Graydon snort. I swear she's acts more and more like him.

"Does he know you tried to kill me? Does he know you tried to take my mates from me? Does he know who and what I am... what we are?" Callie's voice raises with each question. She is standing, leaning over Graydon getting as close to Kelsey as he will let her.

Kelsey ducks her head. "Yes. I told him everything. He's my mate. I wouldn't..." she shakes her head, "... I couldn't lie to him."

"You've said what you needed. I think it's time for you to leave," Zeke says.

"Look she came here to apologize, there's no need to be assholes about it," Liam says.

Callie laughs and not her normal one. This one is filled with menace.

"I have every right to be an asshole. *She* is the one that held me by my throat choking me to death. *She* is the one who locked me in a barn and set it on fire. All because, I have what she wanted... them and a crown. I know I'm not the only one she has wronged, so forgive me if I don't believe a thing that comes from her mouth. And, I especially don't believe this nice act she's putting on. Just wait, you'll see the real her sooner or later."

Liam sighs. "Come on babe, you said what you needed. No need to stick around where you're not wanted."

"There is one more thing. I just want to say that I'm on your side, and when the time comes, I'll be there fighting with you." Kelsey and Liam turn and leave.

"Does anyone believe her?"

"Hell no."

"Not a chance."

"Nope."

You okay, baby?

No. I thought I was getting over what she did, but every time I see her, it comes right back.

It will for a while, but eventually it won't be so fresh.

I know you're right, but today is not that day.

And that is fine. You know we'll be here to help you.

I know.

On a different topic, I wanted to invite you over to my place this weekend.

And what would we do?

I'm not sure. We can study or do some training or just hang out.

I'll be there.

I smile. I can't wait to spend some more alone time with her.

Callyn

Seeing Kelsey rattled me more than I liked to admit. Luckily, we're on our way to the gym tonight. "I can take out my frustrations, with myself, and my anger for Kelsey out on that mat." Lucian reaches across the console and laces his fingers with mine.

"Kelsey will get what's coming to her. People like her always do."

"I know." I sigh. "Does is make me a bad person if I want that to happen sooner rather than later?"

"Hell no," Max says as he pokes his head between the driver and passenger seats. "We're all thinking it."

The gym parking lot is packed. "How many people were supposed to be here tonight because this seems like more than normal."

"There were ten people coming in tonight. This is the last of the new people."

"I think the latest attack might have something to do with this. I honestly don't think people believed us, but Amos finally showed his hand, and now, they're seeing that it's real."

"Go around back and park. There should be a spot next to my dad's car."

Lucian does as Graydon says. We get out of the car and use the back entrance of the gym. I am floored by the amount of people that have crammed themselves in here.

"Oh, thank God."

I hear Cat's voice, but I don't see her at first. I follow the sound of grunts and humph to see her elbowing her way through the throng of people. I smile and shake my head. As soon as Cat reaches where we are standing, she takes my hand and starts pulling me toward the women's locker room. The guys start to follow us, but Cat stops them.

"Not you guys, just Callie. You'll find out in a little bit anyways, but I need to talk to Callie alone first."

"Is everything okay?"

"Girrrlll, wait until I tell you. I'm still trying to process it."

"Okay, you're starting to scare me."

"Man, I'm scared myself." Cat quickly walks through the locker room making sure no one is in here with us. She pulls me over to the bench, tugging me down so that I am sitting next to her.

"Why all the secrecy?"

"Because beside you and the guys, I don't want anyone knowing yet. Hell, I don't even know what I'm going to about it. I still have to tell my parents too."

"You have piqued my interest. I need you to tell me, like now."

She takes a deep breath. "My mates are here."

"OH MY GOD," I yell. "Cat that's awesome. You found your mate. Well, another one. I'm so happy for you. Wait, why are freaking out then?"

"Because dip shit, you're not listening to me. I said mates, as in more than one."

"Oh. Oh shit."

"Yeah."

"So how many are we talking here?"

"Three."

"Tell me everything. What do they look like? What are their names? Can I meet them? Actually, I *need* to meet them."

There is a knock on the door followed by a deep masculine voice.

"Come on out Kitty Cat. You know you can't hide from us."

"Jesus, Stephan is just as fucking annoying as Max. No offense."

I wave her off. "None taken."

"Who the hell is in there with you?" a gravelly voice asks.

I look at Cat and raise my eyebrow. She sighs. "Ivan."

"I told you she was talking to someone in there."

"Screw this." The locker room door burst open and in walks three good looking guys, not as good looking as my guys, but I may be bias. Their shoes squeak as the close the distance between us. The one in the middle is taller than the other two. He's easily six three with short cropped black hair and these piercing silver eyes. The guy on his right is color of milk chocolate with brown eyes so dark they almost look black. His hair is styled in waves that go to a low fade. The last guy looks Mediterranean with his olive skin. His dark brown hair is styled in a mohawk, but it's his eyes that capture your attention. Such a stark blue against his skin tone.

CALLIE!

All four of my guys yell. I don't get a chance to answer because they come busting through the door. The second my guys see Cat's mates they have them pinned up against the lockers, hands around their throats.

"Let them go. They weren't coming in here for me."

"Who were they after? Cat? I won't let you hurt her either," Graydon says.

"They aren't going to hurt her. They're her mates." All of my guys turn and look at me. I smile and nod my head.

"Aww Kitty Cat, why didn't you tell us?"

"Don't you call her that," Stephan warns.

Max just smiles. "I get dibs on the nickname. I called her that before you came along, which was what, five minutes ago."

Stephan growls. "I'll kick your ass. Just try me."

"You won't win that fight Stephan," Cat says.

"You don't know that."

"Actually, I do. Let me introduce you. Stephan, Ivan, Josh, this is Callyn, Graydon, Zeke, Max, and Lucian." She points to each of us respectively. "This is the Alpha Queen and her mates."

"Shit," Josh says.

My guys let them go. There was a round of sorries from them.

"It's fine. No one was hurt." They bend down on one knee, bowing to me. I sigh. "Please stand, there is no need to do that. Why do people feel the need to bend and bow? It weirds me out, and I never know how to react to it."

"It's a sign of respect and loyalty," Lucian answers. "If they didn't do that, I would question their motives."

I get that, I really do; it's just weird to me. "Okay, I'll find a way to deal with my awkwardness about it." I turn to look at Cat and see that she is standing in front of her mates. "You look good with them standing behind you." I give her a wink, and she rolls her eyes. "I do have to say one thing to you boys." I stand up on the bench to get eye level with Cat's mates. Graydon's hands go to my waist, keeping me steady. I fold my arms over my chest and scowl as I look at each of them in their eyes. "If you hurt her, I *will* end you. Do you understand?"

They all nod, but I'll bet it's because my mates are standing behind me more than likely glaring at them.

"Oh my God, you're acting like Graydon. It's bad enough Ivan is showing signs of being the grumpy overprotective one. I don't know if I can handle three of you acting this way."

"I love you, and you're my best friend. I feel obligated to make that statement." I get down and stand in front of Cat. I lean in close and talk as soft as I can. "How are you really doing? Are you thinking about Elijah?" She nods her head. I figured as much.

"I feel guilty. I wished this would happen, but now that it has, I don't know how to deal with it."

"Talk to them; they'll help you. You know Elijah would want you to be happy."

"I know. This makes me miss him."

"That's perfectly fine. You know I'm here if you need anything."

"I know. Thank you."

"Do they know about the other thing?"

She sighs. "No, but I'll tell them now."

As much as we tried to keep our voices down, we know all the guys heard. Damn shifter hearing. Cat clears her throat and turns to face her guys.

"I'm the Alpha Queen's prophetess. I sometimes have visions of the future, of events that are going to happen."

Stephan grins. "So, Kitty Cat, did you have any visions of us?" he asks as he wiggles his eyebrows up and down.

"No, but it would have been nice," she grumbles.

"Not a fan of surprises?"

"No."

"As entertaining as all of this is, what the hell are we going to do with all those people out there? And it's getting crowded in here," Graydon states.

"Let's split them up by taking half of them outside. As much as I don't like the idea, we're going to have to split up too, so we can keep an eye out on all these people," Lucian states.

"My dad is here; he'll help but we could use more."

"I know that we just got here, but we'll help you keep track of everyone," Josh says.

"And why would we trust you to do that? We don't know anything about you." Graydon crosses his arms and glares at them.

"We're Cat's mates. We aren't going anywhere, even after the war is over. Our mate is here, and here is where we're going to be."

"You might as well get use to us. Our mate is the prophetess to yours, and they're best friends. We're going to be seeing a lot of each other," Ivan states, matching Graydon's scowl.

"Whatever. Let's get out of here; we're wasting time and if any of you," he points to Ivan, Josh, and Stephan, "do anything to backstab us, Cat's mate or not, I'll hurt you."

"Fair enough."

I roll my eyes.

Cat nudges me with her elbow. "Let's get out of here; I can't take all this testosterone."

"Let's see how long it'll take them to realize that we're no longer in there."

The answer was not long.

Chapter 17

Callyn

The rest of the week passed in a blur. It was crazy and hectic at the gym. It seemed like more and more people were showing up every day. Cat and her mates turned out to be a God send. They didn't need much training, so they were able to help out with the mass of people. The most surprising person to make an appearance was Kelsey's mate Liam. He wants to learn how to protect himself, so he can protect Kelsey. In my opinion, she doesn't deserve someone like him. He seems like a decent person. Liam's going behind her back to train. She doesn't want him anywhere near here when the fight breaks out. Kelsey thinks he's too weak, so he is trying to prove her wrong.

We've been keeping an eye out on him, just in case he's coming for other reasons. Like Graydon says, D.T.A., don't trust anyone. Aside from that, everything has been going smoothly. There haven't been any more sightings or any word about Amos and Circe. The guys and I believe it's the calm before the storm. Lucian thinks this was a small-scale attack to check our defenses, to see how easy it would be to take us out or get close enough to us to.

We got together with our parents and decided to have double patrols, human and shifter forms. Alcina went to the four cardinal points of the town, north, south, east, and west, placing a protection spell. If anyone so much as walks in this town that we don't know, we'll be alerted. We told the town to be on alert and be prepared. Plus, we have one thing on our side that Amos and Circe don't have a prophetess. I just hope she'll see when they plan to attack. I don't know how Cat's visions work, how she gets them, but if there is any time for her to see something, this would be it. This is the time.

Speaking of time, I couldn't be happier to have today off from training, from worrying. The fact that I get to spend it with Lucian makes it even better. I knock on the door, impatiently waiting for him to answer. When he opens the door, I'm not disappointed. I don't think he could ever look bad. Though, this is the first time that I'm seeing him in sweatpants. He usually wears jeans or workout shorts and he looks good in those, but this, this is something different. His sweats are hanging low on his hips. My gaze travels a little lower, settling on a noticeable imprint. I bite my lower lip, trying to keep myself from launching at him. A note to self, make sure he never wears sweatpants out or in view of other females.

The sound of Lucian clearing his throat grabs my attention. My eyes travel up his body before meeting his eyes. I was already caught looking, so I might as well finish looking. Lucian has a smirk on his face, but he doesn't say anything. I smile and shrug my shoulders. I'm not embarrassed. It's his fault for looking so damn good. If this was Max, he would have said some smart-ass remark.

Lucian steps to the side, wordlessly inviting me in. As I pass, he tugs on my ponytail. I know he loves it when I wear my hair like this. He has this fascination with pulling on it, never hard enough to hurt me, but it's usually followed by a kiss. Those kisses from him are full of passion, full of fire, and I love it.

"So, what are we doing?" I ask.

"I figured we could just hang out. I don't really have anything planned. I just wanted to spend some alone time with you."

I look at him and smile. "That would be great."

"What were you doing before I showed up?"

"Reading." I should have known.

"Anything good?"

"Just rereading a series."

"It must be good if you're doing a reread." Lucian never rereads books. He practically has a photographic memory. So, there is no reason for him to. The fact that he is, lets you know how good the book is.

"It is. I'll loan you the first book on your ereader."

"I'd like that. You haven't steered me wrong yet."

I start to walk toward the living room, but he grabs my hand. "We're going to my room."

I've been in his room plenty of times, but the other boys have always been there with us. I'm not nervous to be alone with him, but if he starts to kiss me I don't know if I can make myself stop with just that. I want to feel all that passion he keeps hidden.

"Make yourself comfortable."

I take off my jacket and shoes. I'm about to crawl up on his bed when Lucian wraps his arms around me. He places light kisses on my neck, pulling me back against his body, his arm tightening. I place my hands on his forearm, giving them a squeeze. I make a move to try and turn because I want to kiss him, but he doesn't let me.

"Not yet," he says in my ear before he nips at my earlobe.

I sigh and squeeze his arms tighter. He uses the tips of his teeth and lightly grazes down the side of my neck, following the same path he kissed. I moan and clench my thighs. I lose all sense of control when he touches me like this, just the right amount of soft and rough. He's back to the soft kisses to my neck, as he stands behind me. All of a sudden, he lets me go and takes a step back from me.

"I'm sorry. I was getting carried away. I looked over at you and I couldn't resist the urge to touch you, to have you in my arms."

I turned to face him. "No, you weren't."

"Yes, I was."

"Did you hear me say stop?" He shakes his head. "That's because I didn't want you to."

"I shouldn't."

"Yes, you should. I want you to." He starts to shake his head again. I turn back around, so I don't have to see the rejection coming.

"Callie, you don't know what you're asking."

"I do, but it's okay Lucian. We don't have to do anything." I feel him standing behind me before he says anything.

"Callie," he whispers. "I want you more than you know."

"Then prove it."

I know what's coming. Just like clockwork, he wraps my ponytail around his hand before he tugs me back. I land against him. His hand traces the path of my neck before he grips my jaw, turning my head toward him. I look him in his eyes, silently begging him to give me what I want...his mouth on mine. He knows it too, by the look on his face and the smile on his lips.

"I know what you want, baby, and I plan on giving you that and so much more."

Lucian

I lean down and capture her lips with mine. Yes, this is what I want. I love the feel of her body against mine. I use my teeth to bite and tug on her lower lip, causing her to moan. God, I love that sound. I take advantage of the moment and slip my tongue into her mouth. I move the hand holding her jaw. Trailing down Callie's neck, stopping to cup her breast.

"Do you know how beautiful you are?" I whisper in her ear.

I let go of her hair, bringing that hand to cup and gently squeeze her other breast. I start to trail kisses up and down her neck.

"Are you sure you want to do this? We can wait," I ask.

Callie shakes her head. "I want this, with you, right now. I feel like I should warn you, I've been with two of the others first."

"I'm okay with that. It makes what I want to do with you so much better. I'll go easy, if you want me to."

"No, I want everything. I want you just the way you are."

"Then that's what you will get."

I move my hands to the hem of her shirt, quickly pulling it over her head, tossing it to the side. I move to the other side of her neck and start to kiss and nip like I did to the other side. Wasting no time, my hands find the closure on the front of her bra, flicking it open. I place my hands on her breast, kneading them but not for long. I take her nipples between my fingers, pinching and tugging on them. A gasp escaped her lips.

"Lucian."

My name a breathless whisper. I wrap my arms around her waist. A second later, she slightly slumps, almost like her knees want to give out.

"Don't worry, baby, I've got you," I say before I turn her around and lift her up.

She wraps her legs around my waist and her arms around my neck, as I walk us over to the bed. Callie starts kissing my neck, making her way to my ear, lightly nipping the earlobe. I moan in response. I gently place Callie on the bed, but she doesn't loosen her grip, so I follow her. I feel my heart pounding, not out of fear but anticipation. Callie feels so good against me, under me.

I kiss her lips, then her neck, shifting down to her breast. Taking one nipple in my mouth, licking, nipping, and sucking, before I turn and do the same to the other. Callie gasp, rocking her hips into me. I chuckle because I plan on getting more out of her than that. I continue my path down her body, kissing along the way. I stop once I get to the top of her jeans.

"Hm, seems like we have a little problem. But don't worry, I can fix that."

I undo the button on her jeans, slowly working the zipper. The sound of the zipper being pulled down can be heard in the quiet of the room. I grip the material at her hips, tugging them down. Callie lifts her hips up, so I can move her jeans the rest of the way down. I quickly divest her of her pants, kissing a path up her leg, stopping at the juncture between her thighs.

I inhale, then growl. "You smell so sweet. I can't wait to taste you."

Instead of sliding off her panties, I shift my fingers, using my sharp nails, ripping them away. I take a step back. She follows my eyes as they roam up and down her body.

"So, beautiful."

I pull back, standing to take my shirt off. Callie's eyes roam over my body. I hook my thumbs into the waistband of my sweats. She doesn't take her eyes off me, watching every move I make. I can tell she likes what she sees. Her breathing increases just slightly. I push not only my sweats down but my boxers as well. Standing before her completely naked.

Slowly, I crawl up her body, kissing a path along the way. Callie's legs naturally fall apart making room for me to settle between them. I press my hard length against her core. I want nothing more than to enter her, to ease the ache that I caused since we began this. But no, I'm drawing out our torture just a little bit longer.

I prop myself up on one arm, not fully putting my weight on her. I slide my other hand down between our body's, groaning as I run my fingers through her slit, entering her slowly. She bucks against my hand.

"You're so wet for me."

All Callie can do is nod. I pump my finger nice and slow before adding a second, twisting slightly, hitting that sweet spot. Using my thumb, I start to make a circle motion around her clit. Her breathing coming out in pants. She's close. Her walls are contracting around my fingers.

Callie's hand finds my hair, pulling on it. Her other hand is gripping the bed sheets. Just a few more pumps, I know that she'll come, but I don't want her to, not yet. I remove my fingers causing Callie to yell out.

"No!"

I chuckle. "We're not done yet, baby. You'll come when I'm good and ready to let you."

Callyn

I'm about to give Lucian a stern look, but I don't get a chance to because he flips me over on my stomach. He positions me how he wants me, ass up, legs almost together, the top of my body flush against the bed. He moves until his legs are on the outside of mine. I feel him teasing me with his cock, rubbing it up and down my ass. He leans over my body, pulling my head back slightly before reaching down to place the most explosive kiss to my lips. He pulls back, and I moan at the loss of him. I hear him open and close the drawer of his nightstand, and the sound of the foil being ripped is the next thing I hear. He leans back over me placing a kiss to my neck. He moves his mouth until his lips are right by my ear.

"Don't worry, baby, I'm about to give us exactly what we both want," he whispers, right before he pulls back slightly and plunges himself into me. I cry out, but not from pain. "Are you okay?"

"Yes," I whisper.

He grips my ponytail and tugs, pulling my head back slightly. He leans down, kissing me, making deep, hard thrust. The sound of our skin slapping mixed with my moans are the only sounds that can be heard. Lucian pulls back; his hands going to my waist, pulling me into the bed, thrusting faster. I can feel myself on the precipice of my climax. Lucian pulls out and starts to kiss a path down my spine.

"Not yet, baby, but soon."

He flips me to my back, settling himself between my thighs, taking both of my wrist and placing them above my head.

"Don't move your arms from this spot, because if you do, I'll have to punish you."

"What will you do?"

"Move your arms and find out."

I bite my lower lip, barely holding back a moan. The thought crosses my mind to move my arms just to see what my punishment would be, to test my limits.

"Good girl."

Lucian sits back on his hunches, dragging his hands up and down my body before settling his hands on my waist. He pulls me up, then slams me back down on his cock. Over and over. The pressure and the feeling are intense. Without a thought, I move my hands down, gripping the bedding. Lucian stops.

"Tsk, tsk. I told you not to move your hands." He flips me back over to my hands and knees. "Now, I'm going to have to spank you." *Wait, did he just say spank?*

A quick smack lands on my right butt cheek, followed quickly by him thrusting into me. Another smack lands on my left, followed by a hard thrust. He does this a couple more times. I'm slightly confused and embarrassed. *Is spanking supposed to turn me on this much? Isn't it supposed to hurt? I thought this was supposed to a punishment... then why does it feel so good? Why do I want him to do it again?*

"You did well." He pulls all the way out of me, using his fingers to run along my slit. "You seemed to like your punishment. You're dripping wet." he pushes one finger in and out of me, twisting the digit. "If I flip you back around, are you going to keep your hands where I tell you?"

"Yes," I moan. He places a kiss on my shoulder.

"We'll see."

He turns me back around, thrusting into me the second that my back hits the bed. Lucian places my hands back where they were, above my head.

"Don't move them. Next time, I'll spank you a little harder."

The thought causes me to moan and him to chuckle. I keep my hands where I'm told. Lucian slowly pulls almost all the way out of me before slamming back in. I gasp, balling my hands into fist, trying desperately not to move, when all I want to do is put my hands in his hair, and run my nails down his back. I feel my climax returning.

"Almost, baby. Just hold on a little longer, and I promise I'll let you come."

He thrusts come faster and harder, almost frantic. I'm so close. Please. I don't know if I said my plea out loud or through our silent communication, but I swear Lucian hears because the next words out of his mouth are music to my ears.

"Come, baby. Now."

And I do. Back arching, bed grabbing, loud screaming, hard.

Lucian

I love hearing Callie scream my name, shaking in my arms from how hard she has come, and I plan on having her do it one more time before she leaves. Both of us are panting, breathing hard. I barely keep myself up, not wanting to crush her with my weight. I inhale deeply, the combination of both of our smells driving me into lust again. But, I know I need to give her some time. I need a little myself.

"Can I move my arms, because I really want to touch you."

I smile. "Yeah, baby, you can move."

"Thank God," she smiles back.

Her arms wrap around my neck, pulling me down on her. We both just bask in the afterglow in each other's arms. A few minutes later, I move and lie beside her. She's so beautiful. I'm the luckiest guy in the world. Sometimes, I can't believe that this gorgeous creature is mine, my mate.

"I need you to do something for me." I'll do whatever she wants.

"What's that?"

"I need you to call out to Max and Zeke, like how we do when we talk telepathically."

"Why?"

"Just trust me." She knows I do, so I do as she asks.

Max... Zeke.

Lucian?

Holy shit. *Yeah, it's me. How is this possible?*

Well, what were you just doing?

That's none of your business. Max chuckles and Zeke sighs.

Give him a minute, Max.

I was just having sex with my mate. They can't possibly mean what I think they do, can they? I quickly think over the conversation Callie and I had right before we did anything. She said she was with two of the others. That means the two she was with were Max and Zeke. Zeke voice breaks me from my thoughts.

We had a theory on how this was possible, and we thought about bringing it up to you but... Zeke trails off.

Basically, if we told you, then we would have had to tell Graydon and none of us were ready for that conversation or the way he would have reacted, Max states.

Anyways, you just proved our theory right. Both Max and I have had sex with Callie.

They just confirmed my suspicions. I look over at her. There is uncertainty on her face. Almost as if she fears my reaction because she knew what was going to happen. But she shouldn't be scared. She already told me she was with two of the others. She is all of our mates. It was bound to happen at some point.

You guys think that being intimate with Callie, taking our bond to the next level, is giving us the ability to finally hear and communicate with each other? I question.

Yes, they both as at the same time.

So, Graydon doesn't know, right?

Max laughs. *If he did, you would have seen the explosion because you know what would have happened.*

I sigh. *Callie and him would have gotten into some big fight, and he would have been pissy with everyone.*

Exactly. So, we decided not to say anything until it happened with you. I take it Callie told you to reach out to us?

Yes.

Is she okay?

Yes. All of us were silent for a minute. *I think we still shouldn't tell Graydon until after it happens for him. I don't want him saying anything that he might regret because you how his temper gets.*

Agreed.

You got it.

Good. I'll talk to you later.

I look over at Callie. "You knew this would happen." She nods her head and looks on the verge of tears. "I'm not mad, baby." I gather her into my arms. "I understand why you did it, and I agree with you. I also don't plan on telling Graydon. He'll find out on his own, when you both are ready." She nods her head but doesn't say anything. I place a finger under her chin and tilt her head up, so I can look into her eyes. I need her to see that I mean what I say. "I mean it. I'm not mad, and I'm so glad and happy that you wanted to take our relationship further. I love you, baby."

"I love you too," she whispers. I lean down and kiss her, then continue to show her just how much I love her, by worshipping her body like the queen she is.

Chapter 18

Catori

Is it sad that I have been avoiding my mates? I'm the first one to tell other people what to do, tell them how it is, give out sound advice, yet I can't take my own. It's not that I don't want them, to be near them, to claim them, but the thought of Elijah is holding me back. I'm not ready to tell them about him, about what happened. I know I'll have to. They have the right to know, but I'm not sure how they would handle it. That right there is the main reason I don't want to tell them. I groan. I need to get over myself, suck it up, and just do it. I flop back onto my bed. Callie should be here any minute. Maybe if I talk it out with her, it will help ease my mind. As if thinking about her conjures her, the doorbell rings.

I roll off the side of my bed, landing on my feet. As I make my way down the hall, to the stairs, the doorbell rings again.

"I'm coming. Hold your horses!" I yell. I pick up the pace a little faster. As I open the door I say, "A little impatient are..." I don't finish my sentence because Callie is not stand on the porch. Instead it's Stephan, Ivan, and Josh. My mates.

Well shit.

I thought I would have had a little more time before they would seek me out. I should have known better. Once you find your mate, it's pretty hard to not want to be around them, to smell them, to touch them, to claim them. It's hard even for me, but I'm made of stronger stuff, and there are some things that we need to talk about before we make any life altering decisions.

"Wh-wh..." I clear my throat. "What are you guys doing here?"

"Now Kitty Cat, you know *exactly* why we are here."

I have a pretty good idea, but I still what to hear him say it. "I don't know what you mean," I say as I cross my arms. I look at Ivan, and he mimics my stance.

"Don't play dumb. Why are you avoiding us?" he growls. I shrug my shoulders. I didn't want to tell them the truth, plus, I want to see how far I can push Ivan. Mostly, because I want to know if he has a gooey center, like Graydon. He growls, and I smile.

Josh rolls his eyes. "Can we come in and talk?"

I sigh but step to the side. *I wonder if I can stall enough for Callie to get here.* All of my guys enter, taking a look around. I move around them and point my head in the direction of the living room. I take the chair, just so I can sit by myself. They take up the couch. For a few minutes, we all have a stare down; no one saying anything.

Ivan is the first to break the silence. "For the love of all things holy. Why are you avoiding us, Catori?"

I shake my head.

"You know you can tell us, right? We're mates. We're here to support you, make you better, stronger. We're not here to judge you," Josh says.

It takes everything in me not to breakdown and cry. I know he's right, it's just something that is hard to talk about. *Okay Cat just do it. Like ripping off a Band-Aid.* I inhale deeply, which was a bad mistake because the air is permeated with their scent. I growl. They smell amazing. All I want to do is sink my teeth into them, mark them, make them mine. I peer over at them; my eyes meeting Stephan's. A knowing smirk breaks out on his face. He knows exactly why I growled, the jerk. I narrowed my eyes briefly, before sighing.

"Fine, but I'm setting some ground rules before I tell you." They all nod. "One, I don't want your pity. What I have to say isn't easy. Two, I don't want to hear any jealousy. And three, wait until I'm done before you ask any questions or say anything. I don't want to lose my nerve."

They all look at each other, and I know what must be going through their heads. The major thing is curiosity. What the hell could I have to say that would warrant those rules? Like I said, once I start I want to get it out. No interruptions.

"Done. Please tell us," Josh says softly.

I look away. It's the only way I know I can start. "So, a few years ago I had met my mate." I glance quickly at them. Confusion, hurt, and anger quickly flash over their faces. I look away, focusing on the window. "Elijah just moved to town, and my friend Kelsey saw him first. She tried to stake a claim on him. She always had to have the best. She wanted the new, good-looking guy. At that time, Kelsey and I were best friends. She was walking down the hall with him, showing him around the school, when she spotted me. I knew who he was the moment he stepped in front of me.

"He was mine, my mate. I told Kelsey, thinking that would be the end. You know, once you find a mate everyone backs off. They know that they're not single, not available. I don't know what changed in her, but she wouldn't let it go. I even asked her if by some chance he was her mate too. I didn't think he was, but you never know. She said he wasn't. So, I didn't understand why she was still fascinated by him, knowing he would never give her a chance.

"For weeks, I watched her trying to make a play at him, but like a true mate he never gave in. I finally had to step in and threaten her. I thought it worked. Kelsey backed off and moved onto the next victim. Or so I thought. In hindsight, she was just biding her time, making plans. She invited us to one of her parties. Claiming, she was trying to make amends for the way she acted. I should have known better, especially the way she was acting recently. But I wanted to believe her, to believe she was sorry. She was my best friend."

I sigh. "We went. I left Elijah for a few minutes to use the restroom. When I came back, he was gone. I asked around to see if anyone saw where he went or to see if he told someone where he was going. It took me too long to find him. By the time I did, it was too late." I didn't know I was crying, and I didn't hear Josh move until he was kneeling in front of me wiping away my tears. I curled my hands around his wrist, needing an anchor to get the next words out. "Elijah died. I learned later that Kelsey lured him there, using me as the reason. Whatever her plan was, it didn't go as she hoped, and one thing lead to another. I will never get the sight of how his neck was bent at a weird angle; how his lifeless eyes seemed to just stare at me in the darkness, or the remorseless look on Kelsey's face. She claimed he tripped and fell; hitting his head on a rock. I didn't believe it then and

I still don't. I had no way of proving she lied. I wasn't there to see it happen, and no one else stepped forward to combat what she was saying. Kelsey got away with it, and I lost my mate and best friend that night. I hate that I may never know what actually happened. It's not that I don't want to be with you guys, because I do. And I'm sorry that I've been avoiding you, but I don't know how to handle this."

I was expecting a barrage of questions, but when I finally got the courage to look at them, it wasn't pity that I saw in their eyes. Instead, I saw understanding, affection, and acceptance. They were all kneeling in front of me. Each placing a hand on me, showing their support. In that moment, I knew I would do anything for them. They didn't have to say anything. Them just being here was enough.

"Were you afraid to tell us about Elijah?" Josh asks. I nod. "Why? We would never try to replace him or make you forget. I'm just sorry he isn't here to see what a fierce, strong person you are. He would be proud of you."

I let go, letting myself cry. I was pulled from the chair and unto someone's lap, but they all kept a hand on me, trying to sooth me. They didn't rush me. They sat quietly until I calmed down and eventually stopped. I looked up, getting ready to thank them, when I felt the stirring of a vision.

Heaving breathing, grunting, and footsteps echo around me. The creaking of a door opening and suddenly a flash of bright white light. The room is bathed in a soft glow. There are no windows, and a lone chair with shackles in the center. The person who was heavily breathing bends and plops someone in the chair. He makes quick work of the bindings, trying the person to the chair. He takes a step back. The person has a black canvas bag over their head. The sound of high-heeled shoes comes next.

"Oh good, you were successful," Circe says as she enters the room. "I want to play with her a little bit before I give her over. She's been more of a problem than what she's worth. I'm so going to enjoy this."

Circe walks over to the figure in the chair, grabbing the bag, pulling it up and off the person's head. There sitting bound to a chair, slummed over, is Callyn.

"Oh yes, this is going to be fun," Circe grins as she yanks Callyn's head back.

"Cat."

"Kitty Cat, come on, come back to us. Did we break her?"

"Why isn't she responding?"

It takes me a few seconds, but I finally register what my guys were saying. "Guys, I'm fine."

"What the hell just happened?" Ivan growls.

"I had a vision. You know I'm the Alpha Queen's prophetess." They all nod their heads. "Well, I have visions. I don't know when I'm going to get them. I get this tingly feeling right before I'm thrown into one. I get this blank look on my face. I zone out. There is nothing you can do. I won't come out of it until the vision is done. Speaking of, I need to get ahold of Callie. What I just saw..." I shiver. "... I need to warn her and her mates. I need to stop it from happening."

I pull my phone out my pocket and text Callie. As I start messaging Callie, the guys start talking amongst themselves.

Me: Where are you?

Callie: I'm just getting ready to head over to your house. Why?

Me: Stay where you are and get the boys. They need to be with you. I had a vision, and it's really important. I need all of you there.

Callie: Shit, really? I'll message them. Meet us at my house.

Me: Heading there now.

I get up, walk over to the stand, grab my wallet and keys and head for the door. I look behind me and the guys are still in the same position they were in when I got up, kneeling on the floor in front of the chair.

"You guys coming or what?"

"Wait, you're driving?" Josh questions.

"Um, yeah. Why not? You see that big, beautiful, black truck with the neon green rims outside? That is my baby."

"Oh, hell no," Ivan bellows. "You can't think we would let you drive knowing what happens when you have a vision, especially after seeing it first-hand."

I start to laugh, and I mean belly busting, bent over laughing. No one joins in. "Oh, you're serious," I say, once I could control myself.

"I've never had one driving, and like I just said, I get a tingly feeling right before I have one, giving me plenty of time to move over. I'd like to see you try and stop me."

"Someone grab her keys."

"Lay one hand on my keys and I'll break your damn fingers," I say menacingly.

"Fine, then one of us is with you at all times."

"You can't be serious?"

"You bet your sweet little ass I am."

"Whatever. It's not like you can actually be with me twenty-four seven."

"That's what you think."

"Look, I don't have time for this right now. I have something of importance to tell Callie and her mates. Now, if you would quit wasting my time, by arguing, can we get going?"

"After you."

The guys follow me out to my truck. Besides that vision I had of all of them dying, this is another vision I can't see come true.

Chapter 19

Callyn

The boys were at my house a few moments after I texted them what Cat said. Now, we're sitting here waiting for her to show up. I don't know if I can take any more bad news about our lives. Is it too much to hope that she brings good news with her? *Stop, Callie. You've faced everything else head on, and you will do the same with whatever Cat has to tell you.*

"Whatcha thinking about over there, angel?"

"Just about what Cat has to say. You know she never really brings good news with her." I shrug. "I guess, I'm just hoping for something good."

Max walks over to me, wrapping me in a hug. "It'll be alright. We've held our own against everything else that has been thrown at us, and this will be no different. You have us, and we're pretty awesome if I do say so myself."

I lean back slightly, so I can look into Max's eyes. He's right, they are pretty awesome. He leans down and brushes his lips against mine. I want to deepen the kiss, but we get interrupted by the doorbell. I sigh and place my forehead on his chest.

"That'll be Cat. I should go and answer the door." I start to pull away, but Max doesn't let me go.

"I'll come with you." I smile. As much as Max jokes around, he's very protective and can be serious when needed, like now. He knows I need support to face whatever is about to happen.

The doorbell sounds again. "Let's go before she gets impatient." Hand in hand we walk to the front door. I open it, and I'm surprised to see that Cat isn't alone. Her mates are standing behind her. I catch her eyes and raise my eyebrow in question. She mouths later.

"Well shit. This can't be good," Max murmurs. My thoughts exactly.

"Come on in everyone."

As soon as Cat enters, she grabs my hand and starts dragging me toward the living room. Graydon, Lucian, and Zeke are already there waiting. She doesn't stop until we are sitting in the last two spots on the couch. I glance back to Max.

This must be bad. There are not enough places for everyone to sit.

Don't worry about me, and they can stand as far as I'm concerned.

I roll my eyes. My eyes flicker between Cat's mates. "If you guys want, you can grab chairs from the kitchen."

"We're good, but thank you," Josh says.

Max walks over and lifts me, placing me on his lap and sits in the spot I was just in. I look over my shoulder at him. "Really?" he smiles, then winks at me. I roll my eyes again but can't help the small smirk on my lips.

"Are you two done, because we really need to get on with this," Cat huffs.

"Sorry."

She sighs. "No, I'm sorry. It's just that what I have to tell you, none of you are going to like."

"Is Graydon going to bear out again? Because if so, I suggest taking this outside. No need to destroy Callie's house," Max states.

"Can you be serious for like two seconds? This is fucking important." Cat looks me in the eyes. "I had a vision about Callie. I should start by saying that I have no idea when and where this is going to happen. Callie gets kidnapped." Several growls and a roar drown out what Cat is saying. Max tightens his hold on me, and I can feel his body vibrating from his growl.

Calm down, so she can finish telling us what she has to say.

My guys don't fully stop, but it's enough that Cat can continue.

"I didn't see who grabs her because she was already taken and being put in the room where they were going to hold her." She takes a deep breath, almost like she is preparing herself for what she is about to say next. "The room where they take her, has no windows, and a chair in the center with shackles on it. I saw them place her in the chair and bind her to it." The guys' growls start to increase again. "I didn't know it was Callie they took until after Circe walks into the room and pulls the bag off of her head. Circe plans on torturing you before she gives you over to someone else. I don't know who because she never says his name, but I'm going to assume it's Amos."

Graydon gets up and stalks out of the room. I struggle to get out of Max's hold, which kept tightening as Cat continued.

"Max let me go. I need to check on him." Reluctantly, he lets me go. I make it to the backdoor just in enough time to see Graydon shift the second he steps outside.

"Graydon," I yell. His bear stops and looks back at me. He turns around and sits, just waiting. I cautiously walk over to him. "It'll be okay; I'll be okay. Now that Cat has told us about this we can take steps to stop it from happening, just like we're doing about our death vision."

"Holy crap. I don't think I've ever seen a bear that big before," I hear Stephan say behind me.

Max laughs. "Well, he is the mate of the Alpha Queen. What did you expect? Hell, wait until you see the rest of us. And if you think that Graydon is impressive, wait until you get a look at our Queen in her shifted form."

I ignore all of them and focus on Graydon. I need to calm him down enough, so he will shift back. I know just how to do it. I wrap my arms around him the best that I can, hugging him. Usually, my scent is enough to bring him back.

"Come back to me my grumpy bear." It takes a moment, but then I feel the size of him shrink and a pair of arms wrap around me, hugging me back.

Graydon

"I can't lose you. I love you so goddamn much. I'll do whatever it takes to keep you safe," I whisper as I bury my nose into her hair, pulling her tighter against me.

"You won't. I promise."

I grunt and can imagine that Callie is smiling at the sound. After a few more moments in each other's arms, I look up to see that everyone has followed us outside. Max, Zeke, and Lucian walk over to me and Callie, standing protectively around her. Callie finally turns to face Cat.

"Do you think your vision of me getting kidnapped is because we finally changed that other one?"

"I don't know?"

"What other vision?" Josh questions.

Cat looks at each of us, questioning.

It's up to you Callie on how much you want her to share with them.

They're her mates. I can't ask her to keep secrets from them. You guys would hate that.

True, but you *are the queen, and she will do as you ask.*

What harm can come from telling them? It's not like it's a big secret that someone is trying to kill me. They were here for the last attack.

She sighs but nods her head.

"I had a vision a while ago that Callie and her mates die. We have been working to try to change the outcome. So far, I have only had one other vision about that night. The sides seemed more evenly matched, and it didn't show me them dying. I honestly don't know."

I watch as each of her mates surround her, trying to comfort her.

"It's okay Cat," Callie says. "You can...we can only do so much. There are going to be things that we didn't plan for, it's just the way it is. But we can take steps to hopefully deter the worst of it."

"Callyn's right Kitty Cat," Stephan says as he strokes a finger down the side of Cat's cheek.

You can see the love and adoration in his eyes as he looks at her. I know because I look the same way when I look at Callie. Like she is the center of my world, because she is. There is nothing that I wouldn't do for her. As much as I would like to wrap her up in bubble wrap and lock her away, I know that's not going to solve anything.

"I have an idea. I don't think Callie is going to like it but it's a way to make sure she doesn't get taken." Everyone looks at me. "I suggest that one of us," I look at Max, Zeke, and Lucian, "is always with her at all times."

Callie's eyes narrow at me. "You guys can't be with me twenty-four seven."

"Wanna bet." I growl. "What do you think your aunt is going to say when she hears about this one? Do you really think she will tell us no? You know that she'll let one of us sleep on the couch, and once we tell our parents, it'll be a matter of time before there's a schedule made."

She sighs and loses the fight in her. She knows I'm right.

"Fine, whatever." Callie turns to storm back into the house, but I stop her.

"I want to talk to you for a minute, alone."

"Go on in everyone; we'll be there in a few."

"What do you want to talk about?" Callie asks as soon as everyone is in the house.

"I know the last couple of weekends you've been hanging out with the guys individually."

"Yeah."

"Do you want to come over this weekend and hang out with me?"

A smile graces her lips. "Why Graydon, are you asking me out on a date?"

"Yeah."

"I'd love to hang out with you."

She throws her arms around my neck, pulling me down to her, kissing me. I growl, pulling her closer. My hands move down her back, cupping her ass, squeezing gently. I'm rewarded with a moan, and it takes everything I have not to strip her naked and take her right here in her backyard. A catcall whistle breaks the moment.

"As hot as this is, and I mean Callie by the way, can you guys hurry it up out here? The rest of us are hungry, and we have some plans to make," Max says.

Callie giggles. "Come on, the natives are getting restless." She laces her fingers with mine and starts to pull me toward the house. I stop us before we walk inside, tugging her back into my body.

I lean down and whisper in her ear, "I can't wait to continue where we left off." I nip her earlobe, and she melts right into me. This weekend can't get here fast enough.

Chapter 20

Callyn

This week has been crazy, and Graydon was right. Once our families were told of the new vision, it almost turned into putting me on lockdown. No way was I going to let that happen. I'm not going to hide myself away. I refuse to give someone else that kind of power over me again. My boys did get their way and at least one of them spends the night on my couch every night. I can't say that I'm exactly mad about that, having them close.

School's going into overdrive with only a few months left. The trial for my stepfather isn't going to happen. I got word a couple of days ago that he died in a prison fight. Apparently, human or shifter, they don't take too kindly to inmates that abuse children. I'm unsure of how I feel about it. A part of me is glad that I no longer have to deal with that, but the other part of me wanted to see him suffer in prison. The guys are happy that it's one less thing on our plates. I'm thankful that Graydon gets to distract me today. I'm tired of talking and thinking about strategies. I'm tired of looking over my shoulder anytime I go out. I just want to forget everything for a few hours, and Graydon is going to be my way of doing that.

Max is the one who stayed on the couch last night, and he volunteered to drop me off at Graydon's. That's not weird, right? It's totally weird. Though I do have to give him some credit, he hasn't made any jokes about it, yet. He pulls up into Graydon's driveway.

"Thanks for bringing me."

"Graydon would've had my ass if I would have let you walk."

"True."

I lean over the console and give him a quick kiss. I hop out the car and run up the steps of the porch. I knock on the door and turn to give Max a wave. Graydon opens the door a few seconds later. Max beeps the horn, then sticks his head out of the driver door window.

"Don't do anything I wouldn't do," he yells.

He puts the car in reverse and backs out and drives a few houses down. We can see him from where we are standing. He gets out and looks in our direction. Max turns to the side, puts his arms waist level, bent at the elbows, and does a humping motion. He then puts one arm out in front of him and uses his other, motioning a smack back and forth. Like he was hitting it from behind. He looks back at us, cackles, then takes off for his house.

I sigh. "I knew it was coming. He was too quiet on the way here."

"He did it mostly for me because he knew it would piss me off."

I look at Graydon and his ever-present scowl is on his face and his arms are folded. "That's not the only reason." He looks at me, question my statement. "Let's go inside. I have something to tell you."

"I have a feeling I'm not going to like it."

"Probably not."

Graydon moves and lets me in. He closes and locks the door. I wait for him to show me where we are going. He grabs my hand and leads me upstairs to his bedroom. He shuts the door behind us.

"Tell me."

"The reason Max was making those motions is because... is because we had sex." I cringe because I'm expecting a blow up, a growl, or some hollering, and none of that happens. I look up and see that he's just staring at me, mouth agape, hands at his side, limp. "Graydon? Are you okay?" I stand there waiting, and I get nothing. I project my thoughts to Zeke, Lucian, and Max.

I think I broke Graydon.

Did you guys finish that fast? You know you have to be gentle with him. He's a sensitive soul. I can hear the laugh in Max's tone.

What happened? Lucian questions.

I told him that Max and I had sex.

Why did you do that?

Well, you didn't exactly give me a choice with all your suggestive moves a little bit ago.

Man, I'm going to have to hide. He's going to kill me.

I guess the rest of us are going to have to hide with you once he finds out about me and Lucian. I think I'm the one that'll be in the most trouble since I was the first.

No one needs to hide, he'll be fine. Just give him some time to process what you said. If he's still not responsive in a few minutes let us know and we'll come over.

Okay.

I walk up to Graydon and touch his arm, shaking him. "Graydon, you need to snap out of it. If not, I'm going to have to get help." I wait. "Graydon, please. Say something, anything." I'm about to give up when he finally says something.

"Who else?"

"Zeke and Lucian."

"So, I'm the only one who's left?" I nod. "Why didn't you tell me? Why didn't they?" His voice rising.

"Because it wasn't any of your business. What happens between me and others intimately doesn't concern you."

"Doesn't concern me? Doesn't concern me? The hell it don't."

"What would you knowing have done? It wouldn't have changed anything."

"*This* is something big. *This* takes our relationship to the next level. You didn't think to talk about it?"

"No Graydon; I didn't, because it was my choice. When I did it and whatever I did with them was *my* choice," My voice rising with each word.

"So, I guess you just choose not to do anything with me."

"If you keep being an ass, then no, I won't."

We end up in a stare off, each of us refusing to look away. Both of us have our arms crossed and scowls on our faces. We stay that way, until the tension between us is too much.

Graydon

Callie gets me so fired up. I swear she looks beautiful standing before me, with her face flush from yelling. Her arms are crossed beneath her chest, which is slightly heaving, drawing attention to her breast. All I want to do is pick her up and bang her on the nearest surface. At this point, the damn wall will do. I wonder how she would take that? I'm the only one that she hasn't been with yet, and it pisses me off. I know it's not logical to think that I should have all of her first, but damn it I wanted to be.

"Graydon, are you even listening to me?"

Honestly, no. All I'm thinking about is getting her naked and soon. I should wait. I mean our first time shouldn't be when we're fighting. It should be hearts and flowers or some shit. That's not who I am, but that's what Callie deserves. I run my fingers through my hair. Screw it.

Before Callie even has a chance to protest, I have her in my arms, pressed up against my bedroom door. She wraps her legs around my waist. My lips are on hers before she can even make a sound. She wraps one of her arms around my neck. Her other hand goes to my hair, gripping, tugging. I growl, and she moans. I use my tongue to swipe at her lips. She parts them just like I want. I slip my tongue in her mouth. I want to be closer, to feel her skin on mine.

I move us away from the door and place Callie on her feet. Gripping the hem of her shirt, I pull it up and off of her, tossing it to the floor. She takes a step toward me, placing her hands under my shirt, feeling the muscles on my stomach. She pushes my shirt up. I reach up and pull my shirt off. Callie waste no time before she is touching and exploring every inch of my bare skin. It feels amazing. Her hands are soft and tentative, feather like. She walks behind me, never breaking contact.

"Like what you see?"

"You know I do."

She stops in front of me, both hands going to the zipper and button on my jeans, making quick work of both. Her hands move across my Adonis belt, gripping my jeans, tugging them down. I step out of them, standing in front of her in nothing but my boxers. I tug her closer by using her belt loops and quickly divest her of her jeans. I growl. Callie looks so hot in her hot pink bra and panties, that I hope she's not too fond of because I'm about to rip them off of her. I inhale deeply, growling as I scent her arousal. We crash into each other. My mouth is on hers; my hands on her waist lifting her. Her legs wrap around my waist, her arms around my neck.

I walk her back to my bedroom door, pressing her back into it. I wasn't kidding when I said the wall would do. I move my hand up her side, stopping at her bra. I fist the front, pulling the cup down, freeing one of Callie's breast. I instantly put her nipple in my mouth. Sucking, licking, biting, teasing. I do the same on her other side. I shift my hands enough to get my claws out, using them to rip her underwear right off.

"Graydon," she says breathlessly. "Please."

I grab my cock, adjusting so the tip is at her entrance. I slam into her and she cries out. "Hold onto me Callie, this is going to be fast and rough."

She places her hands on my shoulders; my hands go to her waist. I give her second to adjust to me. She wiggles. I pull out a little, testing, before I slam back in. I feel her nails digging into my shoulders and I lose control. I start bouncing her on my cock, hard and fast. The sound of her moans spurring me on more. You can hear the sound of our thighs slapping when I bring her down. I tighten my grip on her hips, pounding into her faster and harder. I'm so close to coming, but I need her come first.

Callie squeezes my waist with her legs, dragging her nails across my back. There will be marks, which only turns me on more. I increase my pace, going as fast as I can, causing her back to thump off the door. Then just when I don't think I can hold out any longer, Callie finds her release, screaming my name. It puts me over the edge and I follow her, roaring out my release.

Both of us are panting, trying to catch our breath. I place my forehead on her shoulder as she runs her hands through my hair.

"Remind me to piss you off every time before we have sex," Callie says softly. I understand what she means, but I find it funny to hear her say those words. My shoulders start to shake from trying to hold my laughter in. "Oh my God. Are you crying? Did you not like it? Are you a sensitive person after sex?" My body shakes harder. "Tell me what to do? Graydon please."

I couldn't hold it in anymore, and I burst out laughing. I pull back to look at her face once I get myself under control. "I agree with you; angry sex is differently going to be our thing." She smiles as I set her down on her feet.

"Thank God your dad wasn't home. I couldn't have been quiet even if I tried." My chest, pride, and ego swell.

Taking her hand, I lead her across the hall to the bathroom. "Lucky for us, he's going to be gone all day. I plan on doing this again."

"Oh really? You plan on making me mad again?" I shrug my shoulders. I wasn't planning on it. I want to take my time with her later, but I don't want to tell her that.

"We'll see."

I open one of the draws under the sink and pull out a washcloth. Turning on the water, I wait for it to warm up, before running the washcloth underneath. Ringing out the excess water, I kneel before Callie and start to clean her up. It's not until I stand and start cleaning myself, that I realize I didn't use a condom.

Oh shit. Shit, shit, shit. Fuck, what the hell am I going to do? What the hell am I going to tell Callie? Fuck, what about the guys? Shit, I'm going to be in so much trouble.

Graydon? What the hell did you do? Zeke growls.

Zeke?

Not just Zeke, Lucian states.

Hahaha. Nope. But I am curious on what happened? Fuck, Max too?

How the hell is this possible?

We all had sex with Callie. Since you can now hear and project to us, I take it you had sex with her too? It's the only common denominator in this.

Well shit.

Are you going to answer the question? What did you do that you would worry about what Callie and us would think?

Fuck, I don't know how to say this, let alone tell Callie.

Just spit it out!

I didn't use protection, I say as fast as I can.

YOU WHAT?

I was so pissed that I was the last one, and we got into an argument, and I wasn't thinking, okay. Man, I know I fucked up. What the hell do I do?

You man up and tell her.

It was nice knowing you. I can hear the smirk in Max's voice.

I sigh. I look at Callie, who has a strange look on her face.

"You okay?" she asks.

Hell no, I'm not okay. How could I have been so stupid? I take a deep breath, bracing myself for what I'm about to say and for her reaction.

"I projected to the guys. I know about the link between us."

"Okay, you don't seem upset about that, so what is it?"

"I didn't use protection. I didn't realize until I was cleaning us up. I'm so sorry. I should have done better. Fuck, I don't know what to do to make this right?" Callie is just standing there, wide-eyed, not moving. I pull her into my arms. "I'm so sorry, Callie bear. I promise I'll make this better. I'll figure out a way."

Guys get over here now.

On my way.

Leaving now.

Be there in a minute.

I pick Callie up, walking her back to my room, gently sitting her down on my bed. I quickly throw on some jeans. I grab my shirt off the floor and put it on Callie. I grab her panties, but I forgot I ripped them. *Shit, think.* I look around my room and spot my boxers. I quickly grab those and put them on her as well. Callie didn't utter a word the whole time. As soon as I'm done, there's pounding on the door.

Racing down the hall and the stairs, I fling open the door. Zeke, Lucian, and Max are standing there with concern on their faces. I move to the side, and they all file inside. Once I close the door, I lead them upstairs to my room. Callie is in the same position I left her in with the same look of shock and fear on her face.

I run my hands down my face. "She's been like this since I told her. Fuck!" I want to hit something, but I know that is not what Callie needs right now.

"She's in shock," Lucian states.

"Can you blame her? It's numbnuts fault," Max says.

Zeke kneels before her, taking both of her hands in his. "Come on sweetheart. Come back to us."

I need her to snap out of this. I need her. I swear on my life, I'll make this right.

Callyn

We didn't use protection. How could I be so stupid? I'm only eighteen. I'm not ready for a baby. I have a war to fight, school to finish. I have to finish becoming queen. I love Graydon and maybe in a few years we would be ready, but not right now. What if I'm pregnant? Oh my God. What am I going to do? How are the guys going to take this? This is something that we all needed to talk about, something that we all need to agree on.

I'm vaguely aware of Graydon when he dresses me and when the other guys enter. I feel hands and hear quiet murmurs of reassurances. I'm so lost in my own thoughts that I can't snap out of this. I'm not ready to take care of someone else. I can barely keep myself out of danger. Holy shit, this changes everything. Someone moves from in front of me and is replaced by someone else.

They cup my face. I see a pair of green eyes staring back at me. "Callie bear, please baby. Say something, anything."

Are his eyes watering? Holy shit. Is Graydon about to cry? That snaps me out of it.

"Graydon." One word is all it takes for him to lose control and let the tears fall. He wraps his arms around my waist, burying his head in my stomach.

"I'm so sorry." He repeats it over and over again. "I promise we'll figure it out. I'll be the best damn dad ever." That puts a little smile on my face. I start to stroke his hair. I don't have any doubt he would be an amazing dad. Fierce, loyal, protective, loving.

"How about we worry about that if it happens." I had a freak out moment and I'm sure I'll have another one when I get home later, but there is nothing we can do about it now. I'm putting this on the back burner until I know for sure. "I know I freaked, but I had all these thoughts going through my head."

"That's understandable. I don't think any of us are ready to become parents just yet." Zeke and Max shake their heads.

"If it did, we'll take it a day at a time. No point stressing over until we know for sure. Let's just focus on the here and now, because if I don't, I may freak out again." I keep running my fingers through Graydon's hair. "How are you doing Graydon?"

He lets go of me sitting back on his heels. "I should be the one asking you that. I'm sorry, I fucked up. I should know better."

I shake my head. "This isn't just on you. It's on me too."

"There is nothing I wouldn't do for you or any baby you had. And if happens I'll..." Zeke, Max, and Lucian clear their throats, "... we'll be here for you every step of the way. You won't be alone in this; you'll never be alone."

"What did we learn here boys and girl?" We all stare at Max. "No glove, no love. Don't be silly and wrap your willy. Cover your stump before you hump. Don't be a fool, cover your tool."

I reach behind me and throw a pillow at him before he can continue. He starts to giggle, and I can't help the smile that crosses my lips. In a way, I needed that. This will all work itself out, and I have my guys to help me through this.

Chapter 21

Lucian

A week has passed since the whole thing went down with Graydon. Callie said it'll be another couple of weeks before we can test to see if she is pregnant. I have mixed emotions about it. A part me knows we're not ready for that responsibility, but the other part me would be excited. The guys and I talked about it, and we would raise any children we have as our own. We don't want to know who the father is, well after this time, if it happens.

It's my turn to spend the night over Callie's and I have to say, these nights that we get alone have only made us closer. I grab my duffle bag, that's always ready, and head to the door. I make sure the front door is locked before heading to my car. Opening the door, I put the duffle bag on the backseat. I'm just getting behind the wheel when it happens.

HELP!!! GUYS, PLEASE. I NEED HEL...

Callie's voice trails off. It isn't long before I see Zeke and Graydon in their front yards. I keep my horn and motion for them to come over. They race to my car.

"You heard that, right?" Zeke questions.

"Callie's scream for help?"

"Yes, we fucking heard that. Where the hell is Max?" Graydon bellows.

"Better question is what happened to Max? You and I both know that something had to happen to him. There is no way he would leave Callie alone. Did either of you try to reach out to her?" They both shake their heads.

Callie? Nothing. *CALLIE!* Still nothing. I decide to try to get Max. *Max?* Nothing. *MAX!* Come on, I just need one of you to answer me. Nothing but silence. This isn't good.

"I just tried to reach both of them, and no one's answering me. Get in, we're going to Callie's."

The second that their doors are closed, I back out of my driveway and race off to Callie's. When we get there, Max's car is still in the drive, but the front door is wide open. All of us jump out of the car, not bothering to close the doors, and run into the house. I don't think any of us were prepared for the sight. The living room completely demolished. The coffee table is laying in broken pieces on the floor. The couch is overturned, the lamp is broken, and there are claw marks on the hardwood floor. The list goes on and on.

"CALLIE! MAX!" Graydon yells. Nothing.

I look over to the stairs and see a couple of broken picture frames. Taking the stairs two at a time, I try to get to Callie's room as fast as I can. Her door is wide open and in no better condition than the living room. Her bed sheets are stripped off and lay in a pile on the floor. Her lamp is broken, books and papers litter the floor. Some of her clothes are ripped. Her and Max didn't leave here without a fight. I didn't realize Zeke and Graydon followed me up here until I heard Graydon speak from behind me.

"There were two of them. If you inhale deeply, you can pick up the scent of two unknown people."

"What are we going to do? Where and who would have taken them?" Zeke questions.

"We know who and why. Amos and Circe had a hand in this. We know they want us dead. I don't know where they could have taken them." I look at the clock on my phone. It's been thirty minutes since Callie screamed out. They have thirty minutes on us, and we have no idea where they could be. "Let's start with getting ahold of our parents and go from there. Maybe, if we're lucky someone has seen them. Hell, if we're really lucky Callie or Max will reach out to us soon."

"Is anyone else worried about that? It was like Callie was in the middle of yelling for help when she suddenly got cut off."

"My guess would be that they knocked her out, and I'm going to say they did the same to Max."

Graydon roars and starts to shift. I'm surprised it took him this long. "Graydon, you need to hold your shit. Callie and Max need us right now, and we don't have the time to try and calm you down. Hold in your rage and anger and take it out on the assholes who took our mate and friend," I growl. It takes him a few minutes, but he finally gets himself under control. "Now, we have work to do, the sooner the better." Each of us take out our phones and start making phone calls. In no time, Callie's house is filled with people. The time has finally come to use what we've been training for. We'll go to war to get out mate back.

Maximus

I groan as I wake up. My head is pounding, and my body fucking hurts. "Did anyone get the plates of that truck that ran my ass over?" No one answers me. I look and blink, trying to get the room to come into focus. I try to move hands, to rub my eyes, but I can't lift them. I look down and see that I'm tied to the chair. "I'm all for kinky sex games, but I would like to be awake and aware for them and only if Callie is the one tying me up."

How did I end up in this chair? I rack my brain, trying to remember, when it starts to come back in flashes. The doorbell ringing, me answering, me telling Callie to run upstairs and hide. I tried to take them down, but somehow, they overpowered me. That's when I remember the prick, like that of a needle. *These motherfuckers tranked me. Shit, Callie.* I frantically look around the room but she's not here.

CALLIE! Nothing. Damn it, I need to get out of these. I need to find her. Wait, I can reach out to the guys. The only problem is I have no idea where I am, but something is better than nothing.

Guys?

Max? It's about damn time. Where the fuck are you? We have search parties out looking for you guys. How's Callie? They didn't hurt her, did they? Because I'll fucking kill them if they did.

Geez, Graydon. I don't know where I am, there are no windows in the room I'm in and nothing looks familiar. I don't know how or where Callie is. She's not in the same room as me, and I tried to reach out to her, but she didn't answer.

Can you leave the room?

I don't know.

What do you mean you don't know? I can hear the growl in Graydon's voice.

Well, I'm tied to a damn chair, and I don't know how to free myself. Lucian, do you think I can shift?

Are your arms tied behind your back or to the arms of the chair?

To the arms.

I would suggest, if you can, to get down on your hands and knees and shift that way. Your wolf is huge, it should break whatever is holding you.

It doesn't hurt to try. I'll let you guys know if it works.

Hurry.

That's easy for them to say; they're not the ones with their arms and legs bound to a chair. How the hell am I supposed to get on my hands and knees? It takes me a little bit, but I realize I'm going to have to tip the chair and either land on my side or face plant. At this point, I don't care. I need out of these ropes, to find Callie, and get the hell out of here. I start rocking my chair, back and forth, when I finally tip it enough that I fall, landing on my side. I'm about to start shifting when I remember that Alcina can do a location spell to find us.

Guys get Alcina. She can find us, you know, just in case we... I don't make it out of here.

Don't you fucking talk like that. You fight until you can't anymore. You fight like hell to save Callie. She needs you... we need you.

I'll try Graydon. I don't tell him that, because I can't make promises when I don't know if I can keep them. I call my eyes and shift. The size of my wolf causes the ropes and the chair to break. I get up on all fours, shake out my coat, and let out a howl. Just so they know I'm coming, and they just fucked up.

Callyn

I groan as I come to. I can't believe I got kidnapped, even after Cat's warning. I'm starting to think my house is cursed. First, the whole thing with my stepdad and now this. We tried so hard to fight them off, but neither of us could shift once they shot us with the darts. In the panic, I wasn't thinking straight and totally forgot I *could* shift.

How lame am I? Some shifter and queen I am. I glance around the room. Where's Max?

Is it me or should someone have come to check to see if I'm awake yet, or is that just in the movies and books that kidnappers have such impeccable timing? Never mind, I spoke to soon. The door opens and in walks Circe. I know it's her because she looks just like the picture on Elder Harris' phone.

"Finally, you're awake."

I squawk and move to go after her, but it's then that I realize I'm tied to a chair. "Are you so scared of me that you had to tie me to a chair? Coward."

She backhands me across the face. She opens her mouth, no doubt to call me some rude name, but a loud howl rents the silence. Max. At least he's alive. They better not be hurting him. I narrow my eyes at Circe. I let out a loud shriek of my own, letting Max know that I'm alive.

Callie?

Max!

Are you okay?

I'm fine. I'm tied to chair.

I'm coming to find you. I just got out of the ropes that bound me by shifting. I'll find you, and we'll get the hell out of here. I have the guys getting Alcina to help locate us. I don't know where we are.

I don't know where I am in here. Circe is in here with me.

I'll find you.

Hurry.

"It seems that your lover is awake as well, though he doesn't sound too happy," she says with a smirk.

I couldn't help but laugh. It pisses her off, and I only laugh more. "You do realize that you only have one of my mates, right? That means there are three more out there, trying to find me, and when they do, there won't be anything left of you."

"It would seem you forgot who and what I am. How about I give you a reminder?" Before I can utter a response, Circe blast me with her power. I cry out. Shit it hurts. "That's at half power. Imagine what it would feel like being hit at full power. I think I can handle whatever comes my way."

A low growl rumbles through the room. A large, blonde wolf stands behind Circe. He licks his muzzle, then snarls, lowering his head, teeth on full display. Max. I never get tired of seeing his wolf form. It's magnificent.

"You were saying?" Yeah, I may be getting too cocky, but it's all I got going for me at the moment.

Hang on guys. We found you, Zeke states. I hope they get here soon.

"I've been wondering where Amos is. I thought he would be here gloating."

This time Circe laughs. "The fool didn't know that I was taking advantage of him, not the other way around. I had to let him believe he was in charge when it was me the whole time. He was just a means to an end."

Was? "What did you do to him?"

"I killed him of course."

I wasn't expecting that, Max says.

Neither was I.

Circe moves her hand to her neck, tugging a necklace from her shirt. There dangling is a hexagon shaped ruby stone set in a Celtic star. The talisman. It looks just like the picture in the journal.

Warn the guys Max and don't do anything stupid. We'll try to stall her for as long as possible.

Max walks a wide berth around Circe, never taking his eyes off of her. He stops and sits in front of me. I wish I could run my fingers through his fur.

"Was that always your end game, to get the talisman and all its power?"

"Part of it. See Amos was too weak and couldn't handle all the power this talisman holds. It was rotting his mind, and he was losing the purpose for all of this."

"Which is?"

"To end you and take over. I'll be the next the Alpha Queen."

"The shifters will *never* follow someone who isn't one of their own."

"They will if I make them."

I snort. "Good luck with that."

We're here, just hold on a little longer, baby.

Thank God, Circe is just as crazy as Amos. It doesn't take long before there is a commotion going on, and Circe runs out of the room. Max quickly shifts back and starts untying me from the chair. He makes quick work of the ropes around my wrist and ankles. He pulls me in for a hug, squeezing me tight, burying his nose in my hair.

"I'm so sorry Callie. I should have protected you better. We never should have been here."

I rub my hands up and down his back. "It's fine. We're fine. How about we go find the others and end this once and for all." I pull back, give him a smile before placing a kiss on his lips. "We have a war to go win."

He stands, taking my hand in his, lacing our fingers together. We exit the room I was in, taking a left going down the hallway. We stop at the top of the stairs. Max looks over his shoulder at me and I nod. We make our way down the stairs, ending up in a big foyer. There are doors on the right and left and the front door ahead of us. Where are the guys? Actually, where is everyone? I can hear the fighting but can't place where it's coming from. I nudge Max in the back and point around him to go out the front door. Just as we move, we hear shouting from a nearby room.

Do you think we should check that out?

No, but you know we have to help anyone who is here.

I figured you'd say that, angel.

Instead of going out the front door, we make our way over to the door on the left.

"Stay behind me. We don't know what is on the other side of this door." I nod. "On the count of three. One."

"Two."

"Three."

Maximus

There's a guard on me the second I walk through the door. I don't have time for this. I quickly take my opponent in. He's tall, heavy, and more than likely slower moving. I dodge a fist coming straight for my face. I grab that same arm, bringing it behind his back, shoving him against the wall. I push the arm upward, making it uncomfortable for him. This pulls on the muscles, ligaments, and joints. Using my free hand I grip the hair on the back of his head, pulling back, swiftly pushing it forward, bashing his face of the wall. I let the guy go and he falls in a heap to the floor, knocked out cold.

"Well, that was easy."

"Hey kid, you gonna let us out of here?"

Callie and I turn to the voice. There are four people in a makeshift cell. The the guy who spoke is standing front and center, clearly the leader. He looks like he's seen better days. The clothes he has on are dirty, stained, and ripped. His hair is matted and greasy, like he hasn't showered in weeks. Even his beard is unkempt.

"And why would we do that? We don't know who you are," I say as I move closer to Callie.

"Look, we're in a cell. Obviously, we aren't working with Circe, if we were why would we be in here? That guard has a set of keys on him. You might want to hurry before he wakes up."

"I never said I was letting you out."

"We don't have time for this." His hands reach out, gripping the bars of his cell. "I know who she is," he nods his head in Callie's direction. "She is the Alpha Queen, and you must be one of her mates." I expected to see hatred or anger in his eyes, but all I see adoration, longing. Which is confusing to me. Why would he be looking at Callie like that? I say as much.

"I don't like how you're looking at her. And you're damn right I'm her mate, which means you know I'll do whatever I have to in order to keep her safe." I push Callie behind me.

"I would never do anything to hurt my own daughter."

"Excuse me, what did you say?" Callie ask, stepping out from behind me. I put my arm up in front of her to keep her from taking another step toward him. Callie puts her hands on my arm.

"You're my daughter."

"No, I can't be. My father died before I was born." I feel her hands tremble slightly, before she tightens her grip.

"That's what they wanted everyone to believe. I've been held prisoner for the past eighteen years. Now is not the time for this. I'll explain everything later. Please, just let us out. You have a war to win."

Callyn

There are no words to describe the emotions coursing through me right now. Could this guy be telling the truth? Could he really be my biological father?

"Do you know how I knew who you were?" I shake my head. "I knew because you look just like her, your mother, my Camilla."

I gasp. My eyes widen as I gaze at this stranger. I grasp Max's arm tighter.

"You knew my mother?"

"Knew her, loved her. She was mate."

"Then why did you leave her?"

"I didn't want to; I can explain everything later. I promise. We *do* need to get out of here. I'll help you win this war. I'm on your side, always."

Do you think we should do this?

I don't know Max, but it doesn't feel right to leave them here. What if he's telling the truth?

What is he's not?

It's a chance we're going to have to take.

I loosen my grip on his arm, before completely letting go. Max walks over to the guard still lying motionless on the floor and starts to search him. After a few moments Max pulls keys from the guard's front pocket. Max walks over to the cell door, but stops just short of placing the key in the lock.

"You do anything to hurt her, I will kill you."

"I wouldn't expect anything less."

Max unlocks the cell door, immediately coming back over to me, positioning himself between me and the others.

"Lead the way. We don't know the way out of here."

I do as he says and I go. I don't have time to process this information right now; not like I could even if I tried. This is all too much. I take a deep breath. *Deal with this later Callie. We have a fight to win.* I take off at a run out the front door and I wasn't prepared for the sight before me. The blood, mayhem, and carnage. Why would anyone think that this is a good idea? Why would anyone want to see this; to cause this? No. This needs to end now. I give no warning before I shift and take flight. I let a mighty squawk; letting my enemies know I'm coming. I have had enough. Time to end this.

Chapter 22

Zeke

Has anyone seen Callie or Max come out of the house yet?

No, Graydon and Lucian answer.

Where the hell are they? We could use their help. We didn't know what to expect when we got here. Max did warn us that Circe has the talisman, but the amount of shifters here is absolutely crazy. At first, we thought Circe was here by herself with Max and Callie, but we soon learned that wasn't true. Her followers were hiding, waiting to jump us the second we got out of the truck. What they didn't count on was us bringing back-up. Everyone is here, fighting. There are even some humans here, the few who know about us.

I don't know which side is winning. After I take out one opponent, another steps into his place. I need to keep my mind focused on the fight, but I need to see Callie. I need to see that she's alright. I take out a coyote shifter, then a hyena. A jaguar shifter steps into my line of sight. We both crouch down, ready to pounce, when a squawk is heard, momentarily distracting us. I look up and see a beautiful, red phoenix flying overhead. Callie.

I glance over to the front of the house and see Max, as well as four others, shift into their animals. The jaguar takes that moment to strike. I feel his claws dig into my side. That will be the only blood it will spill from me tonight. The jag swipes out at me, but I dodge. It tries again, but I dodge its claws again. After I dodge its attack for the third time, I go on the offensive. I circle the jag and bite at its hind leg, drawing blood. While it turns toward the injury I just gave it, I do the same on the other leg. The jaguar hisses and growls at me, but I don't care. I pounce on its back, wrapping my teeth around its neck, clamping down. It submits, but I can't leave it alive.

I bite down hard and tear a bite out of its neck. The jag jerks a few times under me before all movement stops. I don't like killing shifters, but it's me or them, and I'm going to do whatever I have to, to get back to Callie. I don't know how long I continue to fight like this, but I'm getting tired, and I don't know how much longer I can keep going. I lost track of everyone. My breathing is coming out in pants. I just need a break, but there is another shifter coming my way.

There is loud whistle and the approaching wolf stops, turns, and runs away. I look around me, I notice the enemy retreating. I use this moment to shift back, giving myself a much-needed break. I also use this opportunity to make sure the rest of us are alright.

Graydon, Lucian, Max, Callie? Everyone alright? Where are you, and what's going on?

We're fine. We're making our way to you now.

I have no clue what's going on.

I just want to sit, but I need to see everyone, and luckily, I don't have to wait too long. The second Callie is in front of me I pull her into a hug, squeezing her as tight as I dared. She pulls back, and I see that she is covered in blood. How much of that is hers verses whoever she was fighting, I couldn't tell you. She looks as tired as I feel.

"Why have they retreated? Do you think we can leave?"

Lucian shakes his head. "No, this is just the beginning. I think Circe is just regrouping."

"She killed Amos and has the talisman. I'm wondering when she's going to use that."

"Who were those guys that followed you out before you and Max joined the fight."

Callie runs her hands through her hair, her fingers getting caught on knots. "One of them is claiming to be my biological father. I don't know who the others are."

"Wait. What? I thought your father died in a car accident?"

"That's what I was told, but apparently he wasn't. He said he would tell me everything once we won this fight. Which isn't going to be until we kill Circe and get rid of that talisman once and for all."

Alcina rushes over to us. "You guys are going to want to see this."

We all run after her and stop dead. Circe is in the middle of the yard, with a white glow surrounding her. Her followers are lined up behind her. Cat and her mates run up to us.

"I wish I would have seen this coming," Cat states.

"Amos is no longer in the picture, and the first vision you had of our death has changed," Callie says dryly.

"What happened to Amos?"

"Circe killed him, and it looks like if I'm going to die, it's going to be here in this random ass yard." Callie turns and looks at Lucian. "Where the hell are we anyways?"

"An abandoned house on the outskirts of town."

"How cliched," Max snorts.

He's got a point. A place out of the way, no nearby neighbors, vast wooded area in the back. It has all the makings for a bad guy lair.

"Not to break this party up, but what is Circe doing and how the hell are we going to defeat her?" Cat states.

We look to Alcina; she is a witch, and if anyone is going to know what she is doing, it's going to be her.

"From what I can tell, it looks like she is drawing on the power that the talisman holds. If we give her a chance to use it, we're all dead."

"So, we need a plan and fast."

Great how the hell are we going to stop her?

Callyn

"Does anyone have a plan?" Cat asks. At this point, I'll take anyone who any idea.

"I have one," a masculine voice says behind me. We all turn to see those who have survived the fight and the four men Max and I saved. One of them claiming to be my father, my real father.

"What is your idea?" Lucian asks.

"Circe is currently distracted. There is enough of us to face what's left of her army. We put witch against witch. One of your mates, preferably the big one..." Graydon snorts, "stays by your side. This is the part I know your mates aren't going to like, but I don't see another way. Callie, you have to sneak up to Circe and try to steal the necklace from her. Once you do, smash it." All of my mates growl. "I told you,

you weren't going to like it, but unless you have another plan it's the best we got, and we need to hurry, because that glow around Circe is starting to fade."

"Real quick," Max interrupts. "Anyone else curious about why her follows have not attacked anyone since we've been standing here? I mean they haven't moved a muscle. No one finds that weird?"

"It seems as if they are under a spell," Alcina states.

"The time to attack is now," my so-called father says. I have to agree.

"Everyone listen up," I yell. "Circe is trying to take on a lot of power. Her follows seem to be in a trance. Do not attack unless they attack you. Everyone pick a follower and wait in front of them. At some point Circe will snap out of what she is doing and so will they. I'm going to try to stop her from doing any more damage. Let's go and finish this." No sooner after I say the last word a laugh can be heard from behind me.

"Well shit," Max says. My thoughts exactly. We took too damn long. I turn and stare at Circe.

"Do you think you can beat me?" Her laugh is maniacal. "I have so much power coursing through my veins I could kill you all with a snap of my fingers."

"Why don't you?"

"Because I want to have some fun with you first. I want to torture you, and I think I'll start by killing one of your mates, but which one," she says as she runs her eyes over each of them.

I squawk. "Yeah, you can hurt them over my dead body."

"Oh, I plan on killing anyone who gets in my way."

"Why are you doing this? What do you hope to gain from trying to control shifters? What did you promise them?"

"Because, you stupid little girl, I was, I am the most powerful witch, then and now. Did I get any recognition? No. The person that I worked for took advantage of me and my power. I think it's about time to get what is owed to me."

Graydon

"I want to know what fucking circus you live in," Max says.

This chick is seriously whacked, thinking people owe her. No one owes you anything. You work for everything you get and have. The way you live your life and how determined you are defines your successes and failures. I'm over all of this. I'm ready to fight. We're wasting time here talking. I need to do something.

Keep her talking, I project. *I have an idea.*

Callie and Max keep her occupied while I slip away. I search through the crowd until I spot my dad. I make sure to keep my voice down. "As quietly as you can, take as many people as you can and surround them. Push them toward us. That should take care of any of her followers. The only thing is trying to get Callie close enough to grab that damn talisman."

"Everyone remembers the plan?" Graydon questions. Everyone nods. "Good, get into position and whistle when you're set. Be careful."

I make my way over to Alcina and tell her the plan. "Did you think you can hold her off long enough for us to do what we have to?"

"I'll try." I can't ask for more. I slowly make my way back to Callie, standing right behind her.

I project to all of them. *When you hear a whistle, it's go time. Alcina is going to force Circe into a witch on witch battle. My dad and some of the others are going to surround Circe and her followers, pushing them toward us. While Alcina is doing what she's doing, Callie and I are going to try to circle and come at Circe from behind. I hope it works long enough to get that damn necklace.*

A round of okays go through my head. Now let's just hope this plays out in our favor. Of course, it doesn't. The second Circe hears the whistle she knows something it is going on.

"You dare try to trick me?" she says as she lobs a fireball in our direction. I grab Callie and hit the dirt, covering her body with mine.

"Fuck."

"You can say that again."

"What do we do now?" Max questions as he crouches down beside us.

"The plan doesn't change," I yell. "You guys use your elemental gifts and try to help Alcina hold off Circe. Callie and I are going to try to get that talisman and destroy it."

I help Callie up, placing my body in the line fire. We stay low, trying to blend in. We use the cover of fellow shifters to get us where we need to go. Only a few feet separate us when a ghost from our past steps in our way, ex-elder Greaves.

Callyn

We just can't win. We were so close to Circe and then the jackass who had me kidnapped and almost killed me shows up. I knew we hadn't seen the last of him, but I didn't think that he would be here, with Circe. Though, I'm not really surprised. He probably stopped following Amos the minute Circe showed she was the one in control and had the power. But we honestly don't have time for him. We have a short window to get that talisman, and he's taking up precious time we don't have.

We need to make quick work of him. We don't have time for this. We don't know how long Alcina and the others can hold Circe off.

I'll distract him, and you go.

"Greaves," Graydon growls. "I'm surprised you'd show your face around here."

"Oh, I came to watch the show, to watch you," he glares at me before looking back to Graydon, "and your mates die."

"You know you can't win against her."

"Who said I'm going to try to fight her? Even I'm not that stupid."

"Then why else are you here? It can't be just to watch us die."

"It's not. I plan on working for Circe once she succeeds."

Graydon laughs, giving me a chance to slowly start walking away. I take a few steps, then stop, take a few more, then stop.

"Oh man. You're useless to her. You have nothing of value to give to her. Besides, who said I was going to let you walk away from here."

Graydon makes the first move, throwing a punch at Greaves. I don't see what happens next because I use that opportunity to run, continuing the path I was on before making my way to Circe. I look across and see that Alcina and the guys have done a pretty good job of keeping her at bay, but I see that they're injured from here.

I don't how to do this? What's the best way to get that necklace? I project to all of them.

Yank it off.

Tackle her.

MAX!

What? I really want to see you take her out and maybe punch her in the face a few times. Better yet peck her eyes out. Yeah, that one.

Screw it. I'll tackle her and yank the necklace off at the same time. I might as well try and incapacitate her since she won't see me coming. *You got this Callie. Everyone is counting on you.* I take a deep breath and make a run for it. Okay, so I don't actually tackle her. I end up tripping and falling into her, taking her down that way. Plus side, I landed on top of her.

She starts trying to smack me. I need to get the necklace. The best that I can, I block her blows with one arm, ducking my head, I reach up with my other hand and grab the talisman. The second that my hand touches the stone, a sense of rightness hits me. Like it was calling me home. I yank as hard as I can, breaking the chain.

"NO!" Circe screams. I'm so entranced with the necklace that I stop trying to defend myself and I don't see her conjure a white ball and hit me with it. I go flying back from the force, landing a few feet from where I was. I groan, struggling to get up. "You bitch. You think you can take that necklace from me?" She starts to recite a spell but gets interrupted by Alcina throwing her own white ball.

"Destroy the necklace," Alcina yells.

The only problem is I don't know where the necklace is. It fell out of my hand when I got tossed by Circe's spell.

I don't know where it is.

What do you mean you don't know where it is? I hear the growl in Graydon's voice.

I dropped it when I got hit by her spell.

Fuck.

Just try and find it.

Great. This should be easy. I roll my eyes. I get down on the ground and start crawling in the direction I got flung from, sweeping my eyes in a wide arc.

"Callyn, watch out," but the warning comes too late. I get hit with something that makes it feel like my flesh is being ripped from side, like million cuts all happening at once. It takes my breath away.

Hold on, angel, we're coming.

I get hit with it again, and I scream. Through watering eyes, I see Circe walking toward me. I should have known this was her doing.

"Did you really think you could win against me?" She stands over me. "I can only image the pain you're in. I'm going to have so much fun watching the life leave your eyes, to hear your mates cry out in agony over your dead body."

Shift, baby.

I try but I can't.

I can't.

"Oh, I should warn you that the spell I just cast, the one making you feel all that pain, is blocking you from being able to shift. I knew I couldn't let you, even I'm not dumb enough to try and take on a phoenix."

The pain is almost unbearable, then I feel a jolt of energy, my necklace warming against my skin. It's healing me. I forgot all about it. I'm the fucking Alpha Queen, and it's time to start acting like it. I slowly rise, squaring my shoulders, meeting Circe's eyes. I may not be a witch, and I may not have magical powers, but I'm going to find a way to kick her ass. I wait until she gets close enough and do the only thing I can, I punch her in the face.

All those days training with Catori and the guys kicks in. I can't give her an opportunity to use her magic on me again. I hit her with a jab, then an uppercut. Her head snaps back causing her to stumble a few steps.

"Did you seriously just punch me in the face?"

I shrug my shoulders, getting into my fight stance. "I will do what I have to in order to beat you. Besides you're using magic against me when I don't have any. This wasn't a fair fight from the beginning. But now that you don't have the talisman anymore, you can't draw on its power. "

"I'm still powerful in my own right. I don't need the necklace to beat you."

She hits me with a spell trying to prove her point and it hurts. I'm so over those spells. I take a few steps toward her trying to close the space between us. The closer I move toward her, the more Circe moves back. I hate this cat and mouse game. I wonder if I drop down if my legs are long enough to kick or trip her up? One way to find out. I drop down to the ground and sweep my leg out, just barely getting Circe, bringing her down.

I crawl over to her, but she's waiting for me. The second I reach over her, she plants her foot on my stomach, using my momentum against me, flipping me over her. I should have seen that one coming. Cat did that to me numerous times.

You got this angel. Get up and show her exactly what an Alpha Queen can do.

I can do this.

Hell yeah you can.

I groan rolling over to my side. There's a shine, a couple of feet in front of me. I squint my eyes trying to see what it is. It's the talisman. I look back to see where Circe is, she's getting to her feet. I make a split-second decision, jumping to my feet and racing over to the necklace. I skid on my knees when I'm close enough, picking it up in the process. I frantically look around, spotting a nice size rock nearby. I quickly pick it up, raising my arm over my head.

"NO! Don't!" Circe screams.

I bring down my arm, hitting the talisman over and over, shattering it into a million pieces. A big, pulsing wave of energy flows out. The force knocking everyone down. I struggle to my feet, feeling disoriented for a second.

"What have you done?"

"Something that should have been done a long time ago. This talisman should have never been made. No one is supposed to have power like that. It's because of you and everyone who has held that talisman that shifters and magic was dying. It's because of selfish, greedy people, like you that half of the shifters here wouldn't have found their mates. You would have had no one to rule twenty or so years from now. Shifters would be gone, wiped out. What would you have done then?" I stalk closer to Circe. "I'm so sick of people like you." I cock my arm back and hit her square in the jaw. I heard the crack of bone. Circe falls to the ground.

"Ooo, you just got knocked out." I roll my eyes. *Really, Max.*

Circe doesn't get up. She's not even moving. I lean down to check on her, to see if I killed her. That's when I notice something wrong with her face. It's sunken, and she's aging.

"What the hell?" I look over my shoulder, seeing the guys stand behind me.

"What is it?" Zeke questions.

"Take a look for yourself." I stand up, moving to the side so they can get a view.

"Geez."

"Man, that's gross."

We all look to Lucian, like he would have the answer. Honestly, I'm not surprised when he gives a reasonable one.

"It looks like the talisman was helping her stay alive, along with the blood magic she was using. Since you broke the necklace, effectively stopping the spell, she is finally dying. No one is meant to live as long as she has."

"Well damn, that's anti-climactic," Max grumbles. "I was hoping to see you peak her eyes out."

I shake my head. I'm fine with that. Maybe now, we can move on and make a better life for shifters.

Chapter 23

Callyn

After watching Circe die, I forgot about all the other shifters around me. I turned to face everyone and saw that they had stopped fighting. They, instead, were staring at me and the guys.

I think you should say something.

Like what?

I don't know, act queenly.

I don't know how to do that.

Yes, you do. Just like the night of the barn fire.

I know what Lucian is saying. Something came over me and settled. I look out, scanning the area. There are dead and injured shifters and humans everywhere. It's horrible thinking that this could have all been avoided.

"Circe is dead. Those of you who came here, fighting alongside her, you are free to go as long as you don't try to pick up where she left off. I will not tolerate it going forward. If you do, I will kill you." Some of them started to scammer away, tails tucked between their legs. Cowards. "To those of you who came here, fighting alongside me, I thank you. You made this victory possible and I am deeply saddened by any lost love ones. Know that was not my intention. I promise to be the best damn Queen you've had going forward." Everyone who stayed, knelt where they stood, and bowed their heads. "Please, rise. You all have done enough. Please, go home and rest. We'll start rebuilding tomorrow."

No one hurried to leave. Everyone stayed to help the injured or care for the dead. The guys and I made our way through, stopping at each and every one person, asking if they needed help. Along the way, we found all of our parents, bloodied and hurt, but alive. Cat and her mates made it out as well.

I look at the aftermath. Too many shifters and some humans lost their lives. As much as I don't like Kelsey, I'm never going to forget the image of her crying, clutching her dead mate to her chest. Kelsey lifts her head; our eyes meeting. A moment of clarity and understanding pass between us. I nod my head. Did I want Kelsey to get her up and comings? Of course. But in this way. I'm fortunate to have my mates, and I hope one day, she'll get her chance at happiness again.

Each of my guys come and stand behind me, placing a hand on me. I can feel the love and support flowing through them. This is the moment that changes everything. The moment we become kings and queen.

Chapter 24

A Week After the Fight

Callyn

I watch as my aunt places a bowl of mashed potatoes on the dining room table. We're waiting for the man who claims he is my biological father. I only met him briefly when Max and I were rescuing him from Circe's clutches. He stayed and fought with us when he didn't have to. I saw him for a few moments after the fight. He told me that he wanted to stay in town and get to know me. Which is fine, but I need to know if he really is my father.

My aunt Dahlia knows what my mother's mate looks like, so she told me to invite him over for dinner. A part of me hopes he doesn't show. You can't miss something if you never get it or had it. I don't want all the false promises of staying here and getting to know me. If he does show, I want concrete evidence that he is my father. I'm going to ask for a DNA test, just in case. I lived my whole life thinking that the man who raised me was my father, my *real* father, but that was a lie. I can't... no I won't put myself through that again.

The doorbell rings and I look over at my aunt. "I'll get it she says. That way if it's not him, I can tell him to leave. I won't let him in here." I nod.

A few seconds later, my aunt comes back, with him. She gives me a slight nod, at least confirming this is the same man she knew.

"Callie, this is Drew, your mother's mate."

He's tall, six foot three, at least. Short, cropped brown hair, and brown eyes that are eerily similar to mine. He's cleaned up since the last time I saw him. He shaved his beard off and has on clean clothes. Drew looks as nervous as I feel.

"Callie," he holds his hand out to me.

"It's Callyn. You haven't earned the right to call me Callie yet."

"Fair enough. I hope you give me the chance though."

"That depends."

"On what?"

"If you'll agree to a DNA test. I don't want a repeat of what happened with my stepfather."

"We'll go to tomorrow and get it done." I nod.

"Please, sit. Dinner just got done."

Drew sits across from me and my aunt at the head of the table.

"Will you tell me about your time with her?"

"What do you want to know?"

"Everything, and I want to know how you're not dead. From what I understand, you left to go get who you thought were the rest of my mother's mates, but you were in a bad car accident and didn't make it."

"I was in an accident, but one that someone else caused. I was on my way back home to get my friends. We had been friends since we were kids, and I just had this feeling that they were meant to be with her. Not only was I going back for them, I was going back to get my stuff. I was moving to be with Camilla. I loved her so much. I had no idea she was pregnant when I left. If I had known, I would have stayed." You could see the sadness on his face. "Anyways, I was on my way home and I get blindsided by another car. The airbag deployed, and I was knocked out for second. Once I started coming around, I felt a prick. I later learned that they drugged me. I was kept chained, locked up, and drugged. I knew who your mother was, the Alpha Queen. I knew what being with her meant, and I wanted it. I wanted her, anyway I could get her."

"How long were you there, at that house?"

"I wasn't there long, a few weeks at the most. I was kept elsewhere, but in the rare circumstances that we moved, my captors would drug me. Mostly so I couldn't fight them, but also, because it made transporting prisoners easier."

"I'm sorry you went through that."

"I'll be alright. I'm free now. It may take some time to adjust to everything, but I'll get there."

I nod my head. "How did you find out about me?"

"I overheard a conversation between Circe and Amos. They said they found you, the next Alpha Queen. By that point, you had already found your mates, and they were arguing about how to proceed with there plan. At first, I thought Camilla found the rest of her mates, but then Circe made the comment that it shouldn't take much to over power a bunch of teenagers. A few things went through my mind at that point. Either, Camilla moved on with someone else and had a child, or she was pregnant when I left. I sat and stewed about it for days, when I heard a guard talking to another. He mentioned he thought Circe and Amos needed to act fast because once you claimed your mates, nothing would stop you. I knew then that you had to be close to eighteen, if you weren't already. The only logical conclusion then was that you were mine. It fit the timeline. When you came bursting into the room I was held in and I saw you for the first time, I knew. You look so much like Camilla, but I saw me in you as well. I couldn't be prouder of you, of everything you overcame and the things that you have and will accomplish."

My throat felt tight from me trying to hold back my tears. I brace myself for the next question. I had nine years with my mother, but I want to know what she was like then.

"What was she like back then? I know how she was before the cancer took her, but a lot of my memories of her are of when she was sick."

"From what I've seen of you, you're a lot like her. She had this fire and spirit about her. She could rip you a new asshole yet be loving and nurturing in the next instant. She was a beautiful soul, and I'm sorry she's gone."

"What about any other family? She never mentioned any to me besides an aunt, who actually turned out to be a descendant of the handmaiden."

"I'm sorry no. She was an only child and her parents were gone before we met."

I lower my head, pushing my food around on my plate. I wish there was more. I wish she was here with me now. I often think about how different my life would have been if she was still alive. I don't regret meeting my guys. Would I have even met them if she didn't die? Everything that has happened in my life is because of that. All the moving, the abuse, my stepdad's downward spiral. Everything stems from my mother's death.

"Once we do the DNA test, and it proves that I'm your father, I would like to spend time with you and your mates. I would like to be a part of your lives."

I look up at him and I can see how much he means it. "I'd like that." Maybe with him around it will be like getting back a piece of my mother back.

♛♛♛♛♛

A Week Later

Drew and I are sitting at my dining room table with a white envelope between us. I'm too nervous and scared to open it.

"One of us has to do it, kiddo."

"I know. I'm just..." I trail off. He reaches over and squeezes my hand.

"I know. How about we do this quick, like ripping off a Band-Aid."

He reaches for the envelope and rips it open. Slowly, he pulls out the letter and opens it. His eyes skim the page before looking up at me with tears in his eyes. That can't be good. It's making me anxious.

"Well, what does it say?" He hands me the letter. I skim it, feeling the tears well up in my eyes. "A comparison of the DNA profiles or Drew Strattan and Callyn Silvers does support the hypothesis that Drew Strattan is the biological father of Callyn Silvers. The probability of paternity is 99.9%," I whisper.

"I'm your father kiddo." I couldn't stop the flow of tears. Drew is up and out of his seat, kneeling beside me in the blink of an eye. I turn and wrap my arms around his neck, hugging him. One of his hands goes to the back of my head, the other soothingly rubs up and down my back. "It'll be fine Callyn. I'm not going anywhere. You really are stuck with me now, kiddo."

I chuckle, pulling back to look at him, my father, in the eyes. He uses his thumbs to wipe the tears off of my face.

"It's Callie, Dad."

Chapter 25

Six Months Later

Callyn

It's been busy the last couple of months. We graduated high school, found out I wasn't pregnant, and basically took over, becoming the Alpha Queen and Kings. When I broke the talisman is started to restore power and balance to shifters. The ones that were hurt during the battle started to heal faster than they normally did, and there has been an increase of shifters finding their destined mates. I couldn't be happier about that.

But today is the day that we're making it official; the day Elder Harris is handing over the reins. It's our coronation. I smooth my hands over my gown. Instead of going with something modern, I choose to throw it back, *way* back. Plus, this gown makes me feel like a queen, and it's how I pictured my ancestor looked two hundred years ago.

The gown is green velvet around the shoulders, down the arms, and the front of the bodice. The cuff of the sleeve is slightly flared and made of silk, like the rest of the dress. There is a filigree pattern on the silk. A fake corset design is in the front of the dress. There are little loops with a grey ribbon woven between and it's tied off at the bottom. The dress in floor length, and I paired it with my favorite black ankle boots. The ones with all the straps and studs. No way was I wearing high heels.

I'm wearing the necklace that has been passed down for generations. The only piece of jewelry I have on. My hair is parted down the middle. Two braids adorn the crown of my head on either side, meeting in the back. The rest of my hair is cascading down my back in waves. My aunt did my makeup, giving me a smoky eye. Overall, I think I look the part of a queen, and I've been doing my best to act the part as well.

One of the things we have done is re-establish Elder Councils all over, with us being the main council. We made it known that shifters can come to us if they feel like their council isn't doing their job. And that we will replace any member if they are found not fit to the job. We *will* not have a repeat of what I went through, not if I can help it.

There is a knock on the door. "It's open." I turn around and see my guys walk through the door.

Max whistles. "Damn, our queen looks fine." I roll my eyes.

"You know, a simple you look nice would have sufficed."

"He's right though," Zeke says.

"Yeah, well, you guys don't look so bad yourselves." In fact, they looked better. They agreed to wear outfits that would match mine or the time period I was aiming for, and let's just say they don't disappoint. Each of them wears a black pair of dress pants and boots. Their doublet colors vary. Graydon's is black, Max's blue, Zeke's red, and Lucian's green. They're all wearing a white undershirt.

"It's almost time. Are you ready?" Lucian asks.

"As I'll ever be." He holds out his elbow and I wrap my arm around his.

He leads me out to the hallway. We kept the old Elder Council chambers. We changed it up a little bit, made it more welcoming. Also, we changed the chairs, or should I say Max did. In the center is a big ornate chair for me and similar but smaller chairs for the guys, two on either side. It's that room that we are headed to. Zeke and Graydon each grab a door, opening it. The room is filled with shifters. There is not an empty pew. Our families fill up the front. We walk down heading for Lucian's grandfather. Once we stand before him, he says a few words.

"This is a day we didn't think would come. The crowning of the next Alpha Queen and her mates. The words that were spoken were lost long ago. Instead, we simply ask for your guidance, your fairness, and your love. To do right by shifters and to make this a safe place for all. We also wish you blessings and hope in many years from now that we watch you pass this crown and your knowledge down to the next Alpha Queen."

He reaches on the table, lifting up a bronze crown. It has fleur-de-lis sticking up all around. The bottom is decorated with jade green jewels. The guys have similar crowns but a more masculine version. One by one he places the crowns atop our heads. We stand as one facing the shifters in the room.

"We promise to uphold any laws we put into place. To be fair and just in any dealing or judgements we may give. We promise to always put what is best for shifters first. We promise to be the best damn kings and queen we can be."

The room erupts in cheers. Man, this is still weird to me. The guys follow me out of the room.

"Now, it's time to partay."

"I think we should take our mate home first and show her just how kingly we can be." I look at Lucian, my sly fox.

"Let's go. We have to be quick our families are expecting us at this get together."

"We can be quick." Max takes my hand, dragging me out of the building and to the car. I giggle.

"Eager, are we?"

"All of us have been thinking about it since we walked in that room. You have no idea how hot you look. Also, we're fucking you with the crown on." And they do.

Epilogue

Six Years Later

Graydon

"Does anyone know why Callie wanted to meet us here?" I ask. Everyone shakes their head.

We got a text message this morning asking us to meet her at the Council Chamber within the hour. We all pile into my truck and head here straight away, thinking something is wrong, but Callie is nowhere to be found. I scowl and cross my arms. I don't like this.

Callie, where are you?

I'll be there in a moment. Everyone take a seat. I have a surprise for you.

Each of us move around the table and take a seat in our usual chairs. Callie comes striding in with two bags. She sets them down on the floor, opening them, taking out a small box and placing it in front of each of us.

Shit. Did we forget an anniversary or something important?

I don't think so, Zeke answers.

We didn't, Lucian says.

Then what the hell is going on?

"Whatcha up to, angel?" Suttle Max, real suttle.

"I have a surprise for you guys. I know I'm excited, and I hope you all will be as well."

I don't like surprises because usually her and Max have done something to me or to something of mine. You would think that they would have outgrown the pranks, but they haven't.

"Go ahead and open them."

Hesitantly, I pull the box forward and lean back, just in case something pops out. When it doesn't, I take the lid completely off. I blink, realizing what I'm seeing. Then I look up at Callie, and she's just standing there with this huge smile on her face. I look over at the guys and see that they are all as dumbfounded as me. I reach in the box and pull out a onesie. In big bold letters it says, *Daddy's Little Ride or Die*, with a motorcycle in the middle.

Each of us have one. Max's says *Daddy's Little Sidekick*, Lucian's says *Born to Play with Daddy* and has a game controller on it, Zeke's says *On Sunday, I Watch Football with Daddy* and has a football on it. All of us are staring at her, waiting for her to confirm it.

"I'm pregnant."

"Hell yeah," Max says then pumps his fist in the air before racing around the table, picking Callie up, spinning her in a circle, and kissing her. Zeke then Lucian follow, doing the same thing. I walk around and stand before her. I pull her into a hug, kissing the top of her head. I release her, getting down on my knees before her, placing my hands on her still flat belly.

"Holy shit, I'm going to be a dad." I look up at Callie, seeing a smile on her face; I grin from ear to ear. Looking back at her belly, I place a kiss on it. My baby's in there. I whisper just loud enough for Callie to hear, "I promise to be the best damn Dad you've ever had. I love you and your mom so much."

I stand, cupping Callie's face, giving her a kiss, and putting as much passion and love I could muster into it. I pull back to where my lips are barely touching hers. "Thank you for giving me everything I ever wanted. I love you so goddamn much, Callie bear."

"I love you too grumpy bear."

Each of us place a hand on her belly, ready to start the chapter in our lives.

Author Note

I hope you guys have enjoyed the conclusion of the Shifter Royalty Trilogy. Though Callie and her guys' main story is done, be on the lookout for a novella about their lives a few years after the conclusion of Alpha Queen. Also, there will be a novella about the night the Alpha Queen perished two hundred years ago and of the handmaiden's journey. My goal is to have both of them out by the end of the year.

I want to thank each and every one of you. My dream of being an author wouldn't be possible without you and your support. It's still crazy to me that people have enjoyed what I've written. Again, thank you. I wished I could have gotten this book out you sooner, but I moved 1,000 miles, from Ohio to the sunshiny state of Florida. Thank you for your patience and understanding. This has been a huge change for us, but one made for the betterment of my family.

I want to thank my husband AJ for your endless love and support. For letting me bounce ideas off you and just simply giving me your advice. Thank you for making sure I met each goal I set for myself.

What's to come? After the novellas, I have a few ideas that have been in the back of my mind. A Jinn reverse harem series, a murder mystery, another shifter series, and one where a girl is greeted by death. All would be reverse harems. I also have a football romance on my mind, but this one wouldn't be RH. So, you will be seeing more from me and I hope you continue to go on this journey with me.

Also, I am looking for two moderators to help with my Facebook and group pages. I'm looking for two people to help me keep the readers engaged and to help bring a little more life to those pages. If you would be interested, please PM on Facebook. Perks include insider information on new and upcoming books ;). I'm hoping to maybe even use them as beta readers. Serious inquiries only.

Oh, I what to give a shout out to Ashley and Stacey. Even though we don't see each other, because of my move, you guys have still been super supportive and helpful. You deal with my snapchats for when I'm stuck and just to listen to me ramble. It's how I work things out. So, thank you. I love you guys and miss you like crazy.

Thank you to Rachael Kunz of Muddy Waters Editing for making editing not suck. You are amazing. To Angela Fristoe of Covered Creatively, thank you for my awesome book covers. They are gorgeous. Thank you, Shelly, Amy, Joylyn, Crisol, and Kelly for beta reading and giving me feedback. Y'all are awesome.

To the readers, thank you from the bottom of my heart. I love you all. Happy reading!

Much Love,

S. Dalambakis

"Castle"- Halsey
"Arsonist's Lullabye"- Hozier
"Over 'Til It's Over"- Zach Farlow
"Desire"- Dommin
"I Want War"- Pastor Troy
"Go To War"- Nothing More
"Bounce"- Emphatic
"Craving You"- Thomas Rhett
"River"- Eminem ft Ed Sheeran
"Hey Mr. DJ"- Backstreet Boys
"Shining Star"- Backstreet Boys
"Ashes"- Celine Dion
"Naturally"- Selena Gomez & The Scene
"Fighter"- Christina Aguilera
"Go To War"- Nothing More
"Far From Home (The Raven)"- Sam Tinnesz
"Blood//Water"- Grandson
"Please Don't Go"- Joel Adams
"Start a War"- Klergy w/ Valerie Broussard
"You Belong To Me"- Cat Pierce

More Books by S. Dalambakis

Shifter Royalty Trilogy
Royals
Queen's Guard
Alpha Queen

Shifter Royalty Novellas
Sovereign (Coming Soon)
Reign (Coming Soon)

About The Author

Hi! I am S. Dalambakis. I am a thirty something mother of twins and a native Ohioan, who just recently moved to Florida. I have been married for eleven years, to a loving and supportive husband. I graduated from Youngstown State University, with a degree in Criminal Justice and Biology. I have been an inspiring writing for years and finally have the courage to release my writing to the world. I have a love for books and all things Harry Potter and "nerdy". I also have an unhealthy obsession with planners and pens.

Come and stop by my Facebook page and Instagram.
http://www.facebook.com/s.dalambakis/

https://instagram.com/s.dalambakis
www.facebook.com/groups/Theroyalpack/

Happy reading!